Letitia, The Rightful Heir

A Sweet Clean Historical Romance

Kerri Kastle

Kerri Kastle Books

Copyright © 2025 by Kerri Kastle

All rights reserved.

No portion of this book may be reproduced in any form without written permission from the publisher or author, except as permitted by U.S. copyright law.

Contents

Prologue: Philip   1
1. Chapter 1: Letitia   8
2. Chapter 2: Philip   17
3. Chapter 3: Letitia   24
4. Chapter 4: Philip   31
5. Chapter 5: Letitia   37
6. Chapter 6: Philip   43
7. Chapter 7: Letitia   49
8. Chapter 8: Philip   56
9. Chapter 9: Letitia   63
10. Chapter 10: Philip   71
11. Chapter 11: Letitia   77
12. Chapter 12: Philip   88
13. Chapter 13: Letitia   95

14. Chapter 14: Philip … 100
15. Chapter 15: Letitia … 106
16. Chapter 16: Philip … 114
17. Chapter 17: Letitia … 120
18. Chapter 18: Philip … 126
19. Chapter 19: Letitia … 133
20. Chapter 20: Philip … 139
21. Chapter 21: Letitia … 145
22. Chapter 22: Philip … 151
23. Chapter 23: Letitia … 158
24. Chapter 24: Philip … 166
25. Chapter 25: Letitia … 173
26. Chapter 26: Philip … 180
27. Chapter 27: Letitia … 186
28. Chapter 28: Philip … 193
29. Chapter 29: Letitia … 198
30. Chapter 30: Philip … 204

Epilogue: Letitia … 211

Prologue: Philip

"What did you just say?"

The late Duke of Wynthorpe's grand salon, steeped in history and grandeur, was fraught with tension. The walls, paneled in polished oak, were adorned with framed portraits of stern-faced ancestors. Crimson and gold damask drapes framed the tall windows through which the pale winter sunlight filtered, forming faint patterns on the Persian rugs below. A crystal chandelier, resplendent with tiers of glistening drops, hung from the ornately plastered ceiling.

Philip John Henshaw, the newly named Duke of Wynthorpe, stood near the lit marble hearth, his arms crossed over his chest. Dressed in a meticulously tailored black tailcoat with silver buttons, a charcoal-grey waistcoat, a pristine white cravat, and black trousers, he exuded authority, though his expression betrayed simmering frustration.

"What did you just say?" he repeated. His sharp voice reverberated through the room, slicing through the thick silence that had fallen after the announcement.

The family solicitor, Mr. Hadlock, a stout man with a receding hairline and an impeccably knotted stock, adjusted his spectacles nervously. He cleared his throat, glancing down at the parchment in his hand. "As I stated, Your Grace, the late duke stipulated that his entire fortune—save for the title—be granted to his legitimate granddaughter, the child born to the late Marquess of Harrowfield, Lord Henry Barrington."

Murmurs swept through the assembled family like a rising tide. Philip, his piercing blue eyes fixed on Hadlock, felt as though the air had been sucked from the room.

"That is preposterous," he bit out. "Lord Harrowfield's daughter—"

"—did not die," Hadlock interjected, raising a hand as if to ward off further argument. "The late duke, it seems, discovered otherwise. According to his investigations, the child survived and has been living somewhere unknown. His Grace's wishes are unequivocal: the young lady is to inherit everything."

Philip's grip on the mantelpiece tightened, his knuckles whitening. "And if she cannot be found?"

"Then the fortune remains unclaimed for a certain duration until such time as she is," Hadlock replied with an apologetic incline of his head. "The late duke was quite adamant."

A strangled sob broke the tension. All eyes turned to Philip's cousin, Aunt Catherine, seated stiffly in an ornate armchair near the center of the room. Her black mourning dress, though simple in design, was of fine bombazine with a lace-trimmed collar. She clutched a handkerchief to her lips, her usually composed face crumpled in despair.

"How could he do this to us?" she whispered hoarsely, her emerald eyes so like her late father and brother's, glistening with tears. "After all we have endured."

Beside her sat her daughter Maria, her rosy lips pressed into a thin line of fury. The young woman's raven-black hair, usually styled in delicate curls, was hidden beneath a plain bonnet. Her black gown, with its simple neckline and full skirts, could not conceal the tautness in her posture. Her green eyes flashed with indignation. "It is unjust," she declared. "We cared for him, nursed him in his last days, and now we are to be cast aside for some phantom granddaughter?"

The other family members—less immediate relations who had arrived out of obligation rather than affection—remained silent, their expressions varying between resentment and disbelief.

When Hadlock finally concluded his reading and took his leave, the room erupted into muffled grumbles and sharp whispers. The enraged family members who did not reside in the Wynthorpe's ducal estate took their leave one after the other, cursing out his great-uncle.

"He must have become senile," Uncle Edward grumbled as he walked towards the door in his stooped gait.

"Surely this must cause a scandal," his wife muttered beside him. "Who has ever heard of something so preposterous?"

"This is an outrage!" Maria cried, rising abruptly from her seat after the door closed behind the last person, leaving only her, her mother, and Philip in the room. "A complete outrage!"

Philip pushed away from the hearth, pacing with measured strides. "Enough," he said curtly, his voice laden with authority. "What is done is done."

"Done?" Maria repeated incredulously. "How can you say such a thing? The title will not keep the estate afloat! Without the fortune, we are—"

"—destitute," Aunt Catherine finished, her voice breaking into a sob. "This... this so-called granddaughter has no idea what we have endured. She was not here to see Father in his last moments. And yet, he gives it all to her? Philip, you are the duke now. Surely you must see the injustice of this."

Before Philip could respond, the double doors opened again, admitting Mrs. Elizabeth Trowbridge and her daughter, Emily. Long-time companions of the Barrington family, the two women moved with an air of propriety and grace. Mrs. Trowbridge, a stately matron with iron-grey curls beneath her black mourning bonnet, wore a gown of somber crepe. Emily, a vision of youthful beauty, looked almost ethereal in her simpler attire, her fair complexion and blond curls softened by the black lace veil draped over her head.

"What on earth has happened?" Mrs. Trowbridge asked, her eyes widening with curiosity as she surveyed the assembled family. "You all look as though you have been struck dumb."

Emily lingered by the door, her pale blue eyes flitting from one face to another. "Has there been some dreadful revelation?"

Aunt Catherine rose, the full skirts of her gown swaying as she moved towards them. "It is worse than dreadful, Elizabeth," she said with a trembling voice. "My father has left everything to a stranger—a granddaughter none of us has ever seen or even heard of."

Mrs. Trowbridge's sharp intake of breath echoed in the room. "Surely you jest."

"I do not," Aunt Catherine said bitterly. "Some... some wretched girl will inherit everything, leaving us with nothing!"

Mrs. Trowbridge pressed a gloved hand to her chest. "How could he be so cruel?"

"It is not fair!" Maria burst out. "That girl—whoever she is—does not deserve what is ours!"

Aunt Catherine sniffed. "I cannot believe Father did this to us, even after knowing my late husband left us with nothing and we have been living under his roof and mercy for years now."

Mrs. Trowbridge drew abreast to clasp the hands of her dear friend tightly.

Aunt Catherine carried on with her lamentation. "I never got Father's approval simply because, according to him, I married beneath my station—a commoner. He did not care that I married for love, which Mama, God rest her soul, always encouraged us to do. Father never hid his displeasure, particularly when my dear William passed away, leaving us in penury. Yet Henry secretly married a commoner, and Father seeks to bestow his wealth on this missing nobody. It is unjust!"

Philip's anger towards his great-uncle flared as the women's voices rose, filling the room with their grievances. Indeed, he had been unfair in the way he treated his daughter, who had returned home to take care of him after learning of his ill health years ago.

Philip strode towards the door, his boots striking the floor with purpose. "This is madness. I am leaving," he uttered furiously.

"Philip, wait!" Aunt Catherine hurried to him, her skirts rustling. She clutched his arm, her emerald eyes wide with desperation. "You cannot leave. We need you."

"For what, Aunt Catherine? To oversee the mockery he has made of this family?"

"No. To fight for what is ours. You are the duke now, Philip. You must claim what is rightfully yours and ours."

"I claim nothing beyond the title, which I realize I do not even want anymore," he snapped. "This is a futile discussion. I shall depart and not return."

"Philip, please!" Aunt Catherine's voice rose, urgent and distressed. She reached for his arm again, stopping him mid-step. "You cannot abandon us now. We have no one else."

He turned slowly, his expression guarded. "And what would you have me do, Aunt?"

"You must help us," she implored. "*You* are the duke. You have the power to claim what is lawfully ours."

"What you ask is impossible."

"It is not!" Maria interjected, her face flushed with anger. "Do you expect us to simply leave, then? Where will we go? What will we do?"

He sighed as he stared at his cousins. "I shall take care of the both of you. You have my word."

"And leave a stranger to claim what belongs to us?" she threw at him. "You are the head of this family now, Philip. You must act like it."

Philip sighed, not liking the burden of their expectations pressing down on him. He glanced at Mrs. Trowbridge, who was regarding him with a shrewd, calculating gaze.

"She is right," Mrs. Trowbridge said firmly. "You have a duty, Your Grace. To your cousins."

Emily nodded. "Surely you cannot let the late duke's... misguided decision ruin the family."

Aunt Catherine dabbed at her eyes dramatically. "Please, Philip. Do not abandon us. Not now."

He exhaled softly, running a hand through his black hair. He had little interest in inheritance disputes, but his loyalty to the Barringtons was not something he could easily cast aside.

"Very well then. I shall stay and see it through. But mark my words, I will not be party to deceit or sabotage."

Maria scoffed. "That is noble of you, Philip. But it will not keep us fed."

Aunt Catherine clasped her hands together in relief. "Thank you, Philip. All we ask is that you help us find this girl. If she truly is Father's granddaughter, then so be it. But if she is not..." she trailed off, letting the implication hang in the air.

Philip frowned at the suggestion, but he nodded stiffly. "Very well."

Maria, however, did not look appeased. "It is not enough to simply find her," she said darkly. "She must be shown that she does not belong here."

He felt a twinge of unease at her words but said nothing.

"Good," Mrs. Trowbridge said with a satisfied smile. "Then it is settled. We shall find this so-called heiress. And we shall see if she is fit to inherit anything at all."

As the women resumed their quiet plotting, Philip moved to the window, staring out at the frost-covered grounds. A storm of emotions rose in his chest—rage at his great-uncle's betrayal, despair at his family's plight, and an unease he could not quite name. He had been engulfed with mixed feelings when the late duke had announced that he, a distant cousin, was to inherit the title as he was the closest male relative—the deceased man had no sons, grandsons, or nephews. If he had known it would be this much trouble, he would have rejected the offer and allowed it to pass on to his immediate younger brother, James.

The portrait of his great-uncle, hanging above the hearth, seemed to mock him.

"You have left us with quite the mess, old man," Philip murmured. "And I shall see it set right. One way or another."

He silently vowed to himself. *I shall do what must be done. For the family. For Wynthorpe.*

Chapter 1: Letitia

"I am sorry, I cannot marry you, Andrew."

Letitia stood with her hands clasped before her in the meadow, her bonnet shielding her face from the sun's brilliance. Before her stood Andrew Hargrove, his face earnest.

"Letitia," he called gently, his voice shaking with emotion. "You must know how much I care for you. Marry me, and I promise to make you happy."

Letitia's heart ached for the man before her. Andrew was a kind and loyal friend, a man who deserved a wife who could return his love. Yet, she could not give him what he sought.

"Andrew," she began softly, "you are a dear friend, but I cannot accept your proposal. My heart... it does not feel for you as yours does for me."

His face became pale, his broad shoulders sagging. "But surely love can grow, Letitia," he implored with a raised hand of supplication, his brown eyes pleading. "We have known each other for years and have been good friends. Is that not a foundation for something more?"

She took a step back. "You deserve someone who will love you wholly, and that is not me. I think of you as a brother, Andrew. To marry you would not be fair to either of us."

"You could learn to love me as your husband," he insisted.

She shook her head gently. "A marriage without love is not one I can abide."

He looked away, his hand falling to his side. "I had hoped," he said with disappointment. "But I see now that hope was misplaced."

"I am truly sorry," she said, her heart sinking at the pain etched on his freckled face.

The sound of thundering hooves broke the solemn atmosphere. Letitia turned to see her younger sister, Frances, galloping towards them on a chestnut mare. Her riding habit, though slightly dusty, flattered her lithe figure, and her untamed curls framed her youthful face beneath her bonnet.

"Lettie!" Frances called, reigning in her horse with practiced ease. "Mama says she needs to speak with you urgently."

Letitia nodded, turning back to Andrew. "Goodbye, Andrew," she said softly.

He gave a small bow, his gaze lingering on her for a moment before he turned and walked away towards the village.

Frances frowned as Letitia mounted a bay mare. "What was that about?"

Letitia shook her head. "Nothing to concern yourself with, Fran." There was no need for anyone else to know how she had broken poor Andrew's heart with unrequited feelings.

Frances wrinkled her button nose for a moment and then a mischievous glint appeared in her brown eyes. "Shall we race back home?"

Letitia smiled. "Very well. But do not think you will beat me so easily this time!"

Frances let out a delighted laugh and spurred her mare into a gallop, her laughter carried on the breeze. Letitia urged her horse forward, the thrill of the chase pushing the heaviness of her earlier conversation aside.

The village of Brookstone came into view, a cluster of quaint stone cottages set among rolling hills. Smoke curled lazily from chimneys, and the brook that gave the village its name sparkled in the sunlight as it meandered through the fields. Children played along the dirt paths, their laughter adding to the cheerful scene. The scent of wildflowers filled the air as they raced past fields bordered by dry stone walls.

Frances reached the gate of their small cottage first, her cheeks flushed with triumph. "I win again!" she declared, sliding off her horse and patting its neck.

Letitia dismounted, shaking her head in mock exasperation. "One day, Fran, I shall surprise you."

Frances took the mare's reins from her sister. "Shall I rub them down before returning them to Daniel? He will be wanting them back soon."

"Thank you," Letitia said, walking away. Their younger brothers, Daniel and Thomas, worked as stable lads for Lord Bannerman. The lads allowed their sisters to borrow some horses and exercise them once a week.

The cottage, with its ivy-covered walls and neatly tended garden with vibrant colors, was a comforting sight. The chickens clucked contentedly in their coop while the goats and sheep grazed nearby.

Inside, the sitting room was modest but cozy, with a settee, a well-worn armchair near the fireplace, and shelves lined with books and trinkets. A faded rug softened the stone floor, and sunlight filtered through the lace curtains.

Her mother, Helen Robinson, sat in the armchair clutching a newspaper. Her plain grey gown was unadorned, her brown hair covered in a white bonnet. She looked up as Letitia entered, her face tight with worry.

"Come, sit down, Lettie."

Alarm prickled Letitia's senses as she crossed the room and sat on the wooden chair opposite her. "What is it, Mama?"

The older woman's gaze wavered, her hands quivering as she clutched the paper. Tears filled her honey-brown eyes.

"I must beg your forgiveness," she said with anguish.

"Forgiveness? Whatever for?"

"For keeping the truth from you all these years," she whispered. "I did it to protect you, my dear, from those who wished you harm."

Letitia stared at her, uncomprehending. "I do not understand."

"I have something to tell you, my dear. Something I should have told you long ago."

Letitia's heart quickened. "What do you mean?"

She took a shuddering breath. "I am not your mother, Lettie. I am your aunt. Your mother—my sister—died shortly after you were born."

The words struck Letitia like a blow. "That cannot be true," Letitia whispered, shaking her head in disbelief.

"It is," she said, her tears spilling over her round face. "Your mother fell in love with the Marquess of Harrowfield, but his father, the Duke of Wynthorpe, disapproved of the match. So, they married in secret. When you were born, your mother..." Her voice broke, and she pressed a hand to her lips. "She died only days later."

Letitia stared at her with incredulity. "What? Why have you never told me this?"

"Because it was too dangerous," she rasped. She recounted the harrowing tale of a maid's attempt to smother Letitia as an infant, the flight to Brookstone, and the life she had built to keep her niece safe.

"I had to protect you from whoever in your father's family wanted you dead, and the only way to do that was to take you far away and pretend you were my daughter. When I met your papa... that is my husband, Benjamin, and told him everything, he was very understanding. We got married and raised you as our child."

Letitia felt as if she was in a bad dream that she would soon wake from. How could this be possible? That the woman she had always called her mother is actually her aunt? So, Frances, Daniel, and Thomas are her cousins? And Papa is her aunt's husband?

With her heart thundering in disbelief, she raised her confused emerald eyes and asked, "Why are you telling me this now? Do you wish to send me away?"

She paled instantly. "Of course not! I would never do that, my dear." She handed Letitia the newspaper. The headline read: *Duke's Family Seeks Missing Heiress.*

With shaking hands, she read that the family of the Duke of Wynthorpe were looking for their missing granddaughter, born twenty years ago, to come and claim her inheritance.

Letitia lifted her troubled gaze from the paper. "What does this mean?"

Her aunt's tear-streaked face was a portrait of regret. "They are searching for you. Your father's family. You are their heiress."

Letitia stood abruptly, the chair scraping against the floor. "No! This cannot be true!"

"It is," she whispered. "You are indeed the granddaughter of the late Duke of Wynthorpe."

Unable to bear the revelation, Letitia turned and fled the room, her vision blurred with tears. She ran to the pond at the edge of the village, the one place where she could always find solace. The water sparkled in the sunlight, framed by reeds and wildflowers.

She sank to her knees, her sobs wracking her frame. Her life felt like a cruel lie, her very identity stripped away. How could her mother... aunt have kept such a thing from her?

Who am I? she wondered with despair. Now she understood why she was the only one in the family who had emerald eyes. Her mother... her aunt had spawned a tale about their grandmother, but now she realized she must have gotten her eye color from her father's family. Who were they? These people whose genealogy she shared?

How can I ever come to terms with this? That I do not belong to the family I have always known?

"I am an outsider," she whispered brokenly.

Footsteps approached, and she turned to see Frances. Her sister's... cousin's usually bright eyes were red-rimmed and her demeanor solemn.

"I heard everything," Frances confessed, sitting beside her.

Fresh tears spilled down Letitia's cheeks as Frances wrapped her arms around her. "You are my sister," Frances said fiercely. "Nothing will change that."

Letitia clung to her, her heart aching with gratitude. "Thank you," she whispered.

They stayed in companionable silence for a while as Letitia wondered what she would do now. It was obvious her mother... aunt wanted her to go to her father's family, hence the reason for telling her, but she could not. How could she leave the only home she had ever known to go and be with strangers, real family or not?

Frances managed a small smile a while later, her teasing nature emerging despite the situation. "Look on the bright side. You must admit, 'tis rather exciting. You are a lady now! My, the daughter of a duke. Who would have thought...?"

Letitia shook her head vehemently. "This is my home, Frances. I belong here, with you and our family. I go nowhere."

In the days that followed the revelation, Letitia avoided her aunt, immersing herself in chores away from the house to keep her mind from the turmoil. She took her time to feed the hens, fetch water from the brook, milk the cow, and take the goats and sheep further out to pasture. She stayed with them until late in the day before herding them back. Her aunt never said a word but watched her with sad eyes, which Letitia tried to avoid.

One morning, while Letitia was scrubbing clothes by the brook with a vengeance as if they were the source of her ordeal, the man she had always called *Papa* approached. His weathered face was filled with concern.

"Lettie, I know you feel wretched right now with the change in your situation, but you are hurting your mother," he said gently.

She is not my mother, Letitia almost shouted, but she stayed her tongue, not intending to cause hurt.

"She did what she thought was best for you."

Tears welled in Letitia's eyes. "My whole life has been a lie. How can I forgive that?"

"Because she loves you as her own," he said calmly. "Because she gave you a life when others sought to take it away. She will always be your mother in every way that matters."

His words broke through her defenses, and she sobbed into his arms. "Thank you, Papa."

"There, there." He patted her head.

She sniffed. "And thank you for giving me a home, even when I am not your daughter."

"You will always be my daughter."

Later, she returned to the cottage and found her aunt in the sitting room. The older woman looked up with guilt and sorrow.

"I am so sorry, Lettie."

Letitia crossed the room and embraced her tightly. "I understand," she said as tears spilled down her face. "You did what you thought was best."

Aunt Helen pulled back and cupped her face. "You must go to London."

"No," she replied firmly. "My life is here."

"You must claim your inheritance. Meet your father's family."

She shook her head, the thought of leaving her home terrifying. "I do not think I can, Mama."

"Yes, you can."

"But why should I go to the people who tried to kill me?"

"Your grandfather, who I suspect was the culprit, is dead now, although the maid refused to tell me who sent her, as she was afraid for her life. So, you have nothing to fear."

A frown contorted her face. "But if he tried to have me killed, why would he then name me as his heiress?"

Her aunt shrugged. "Mayhap remorse. Your father died without an heir."

Letitia sighed heavily. "I shall think about it."

"Please do. But we must make haste. The paper is dated three months ago."

Letitia nodded and went to the room she shared with Frances. A part of her wanted her to go. After all, she had always longed to travel and see the world outside the small village, but another part was frightened. What if she was not accepted? What if someone tried to kill her again?

But as hours turned into days, she warmed up to the idea of seeing another part of life. Had she not always wondered when she read books or walked past Lord Bannerman's house what it would feel like to be a lady and surrounded by wealth and opulence?

In the end, she agreed to go and accepted that her life was about to change forever.

Chapter 2: Philip

The drawing room of the Duke of Wynthorpe's townhouse in London had never felt so suffocating. Philip stood by the grand window, his gaze absently tracking the carriages rattling along the cobbled street outside. The morning sunbeams streamed in, highlighting the impeccable elegance of the room with its sumptuous drapery and a cluster of upholstered chairs gathered near the hearth. Despite the grandeur, Philip felt the sharp prick of frustration gnawing at his temper.

"Another imposter," he said, running a hand through his hair, the sheen of annoyance glinting in his blue eyes. He turned from the window and strode to a corner of the room, where a decanter of brandy and several glasses awaited. Pouring himself a measure, he glanced at the assembled company.

Seated nearest to him was Aunt Catherine, her hair swept into an elegant chignon, her face as calm as marble. Beside her, Mrs. Trowbridge, with her sharp features and a penchant for gossip, nodded sympathetically. Emily, slim and pretty in a pale blue muslin gown, sat demurely with her hands folded. Maria was perched on the settee beside her mother, brow furrowed.

Philip took a sip of his brandy, savoring the warmth as it slid down his throat, and set the glass down with a decisive clink. "This is the fifth one," he announced, irritation sharpening his tone at the memory of the young woman they just sent away. "Five women in three months, all claiming to be the missing granddaughter. And every single one has turned out to be a charlatan. If I see one more lady with some hastily concocted tale, I may lose my temper altogether."

Aunt Catherine raised her fan and flicked it open with a practiced ease, though her voice carried an edge of weariness. "It is to be expected. Sometimes I wish we had not made it public, but we did not have a choice. When one places an announcement of such import in the papers, the vultures are bound to circle."

"Vultures?" Mrs. Trowbridge sniffed with disdain. "More like clumsy sparrows. The last one could barely keep her story straight."

Emily chuckled softly, though her laughter faltered when Philip fixed her with a pointed look.

"The private investigator was a waste of resources," he continued. "Three months and not a shred of useful information. Only that the girl's aunt spirited her away years ago, never to be seen again. I cannot fathom why we persist."

"Because we must," Aunt Catherine said firmly. "Maria and I have no claim to the estate unless the rightful heiress is found, or proven deceased."

With mounting anger, Philip recalled the four previous ladies who had arrived pretending to be the missing granddaughter; they were eventually caught because they were in cahoots with some servants. And so, they had had to dismiss all the servants and hire new ones who did not know about the duke's will.

He gritted his teeth. "Three months of fraudsters, gossipmongers, and every manner of scandal-loving busybody plaguing my steps. Wherever I go—White's, the park, even my tailor—someone must ask, *'Have you found the lost heiress yet, Your Grace?'* It is insufferable!"

"You did agree to assist," Mrs. Trowbridge reminded him with a wry smile.

Emily glanced up from the pianoforte where she had been absently tapping at the keys. Her blonde curls framed a delicate face that displayed both amusement and sympathy. "It *is* quite the ordeal, Philip dear, but think of the grand tale it will make once the rightful heiress is found."

Maria's eyes filled with skepticism. "If she is found," she murmured.

Philip turned sharply. "Must you always be so bleak, Maria?"

"I am not bleak," she retorted, smirking. "Merely pragmatic. And so far, pragmatism has been the correct outlook."

Before Philip could retort, the drawing room door swung open. The new butler, Mr. Forbes, entered the room and bowed. His usually impassive face showed a trace of discomfort. "Forgive the interruption, Your Grace, but there is a young woman in the foyer claiming to be the late duke's granddaughter. Two ladies accompany her."

Philip groaned, pinching the bridge of his nose. "Another one so soon?"

"Shall I send them away?" Forbes inquired.

"Send her in, then. Let us be done with this nonsense."

The butler bowed and departed, leaving the room in tense anticipation.

Aunt Catherine raised her brows. "Philip, do try to be civil."

He gave her a look that clearly conveyed his thoughts on that suggestion but did not reply. She obviously did not understand how frustrated he was and how much he wished he could excuse himself from it all. But he had a duty to fulfill.

A moment later, the doors opened again, and three figures entered. The first was a middle-aged woman of modest appearance, her posture stiff but with an air of resolute dignity. Beside her, a fresh-faced younger version of the older woman in a plain blue dress and with lively eyes took in the room with evident curiosity. He shifted his gaze past her to the third woman and remained there. She was perhaps of eighteen years, clad in a simple yet elegant gown of deep green muslin, the rich color enhancing her fair complexion. The simple cut of the dress, with its high neckline and unembellished hem, only served to highlight her natural beauty and her slightly curvy frame. Though the gown was modest, her posture was regal, her steps unhurried, and her head held high.

Philip's breath caught involuntarily as his initial annoyance wavered. She was striking, with raven black hair swept into a neat knot at her nape, a few loose curls framing a heart-shaped face underneath her bonnet. Her eyes, a rich shade of emerald, held a combination of boldness and composure. She wriggled her pointed nose as if with distaste, and her rosebud lips formed a stiff smile. There was an understated grace about her, a regal bearing that none of the previous pretenders had possessed.

Her beauty was undeniable, but it was her attitude that gave him pause. She carried herself not like a charlatan eager to please, but with the poise of someone who knew her worth.

Still, Philip forced himself to focus. Beauty and poise had nothing to do with the truth, and appearances would not sway him.

"Another one?" he drawled, his tone laced with skepticism. "And what tale shall we hear today? Lost at sea all this while? Raised by wolves?"

The young woman met his gaze, unflinching. "Neither," she replied evenly, her voice tinged with wry amusement. "But if it will entertain you, I am happy to oblige."

He blinked, momentarily thrown by her quick wit. He recovered swiftly, his expression hardening. "You presume much, Miss, by coming here to claim a title that might not be yours."

"And you presume, sir," she countered, "to judge me without the courtesy of hearing what I have to say."

He let out a derisive snort. "And what evidence do you bring to claim such an illustrious heritage?"

She arched a brow at his condescending tone. "Evidence? Forgive me, but do you expect me to carry a family tree in my reticule?"

The women of his household gasped at the young woman's effrontery.

Philip's eyes narrowed. He was not accustomed to being spoken to with such boldness by a woman, not even before he became a duke. "I expect you to bring more than mere audacity," he retorted.

"And yet," she said smoothly, "it seems audacity is what this household needs. From what I hear, you have been duped by no fewer than four false claimants already. Perhaps the fault lies not with the seekers but with the gatekeepers."

The room went silent, save for Maria's muffled gasp.

Philip's temper ignited. "How dare you—"

"How dare I speak plainly?" she interrupted. "Quite easily. It seems someone must, given the situation."

He took a step forward, his height towering over her, but she did not flinch. Her gaze remained locked with his. There was a flicker of something familiar in her eyes, but he quickly dismissed it.

"You are bold, Miss, but boldness is no substitute for truth."

"Nor is arrogance a substitute for wit," she shot back.

Before he could respond, Aunt Catherine cleared her throat, her sharp gaze darting between them. "Enough, Philip. Allow the lady to speak."

"Very well," he said tightly, gesturing for them to sit.

The older woman began, her hands folded neatly in front of her. "I am Helen Robinson. This is my daughter, Frances. And this is my niece, Miss... er... Lady Letitia Barrington, the late duke's granddaughter and rightful heiress."

Philip arched a brow. "And I presume you have evidence of this remarkable claim?"

"Indeed," Mrs. Robinson replied. "We have letters from the late Lord Harrowfield addressed to Letitia's mother—my late sister—as well as several personal effects that belonged to the family. Furthermore, Letitia bears a striking resemblance to her mother and has some features of her father."

Philip turned his attention back to Letitia, studying her closely. Now that her aunt had mentioned it, there was a faint familiarity about her features. She also had emerald eyes like the Barringtons. But he refused to let his guard down. Two of the other fraudsters had also sported the same eye color.

"And you, Miss Letitia," he said, his tone clipped. "What say you to this supposed resemblance?"

Letitia tilted her chin, her emerald eyes narrowing. "I would say, my lord—"

"Your Grace," he interrupted sharply.

He enjoyed her brief moment of fluster before she nodded and carried on. "I beg your pardon... *Your Grace*, that it is a poor defense to accuse a lady of fabrication when she has yet to present her case."

A smirk tugged at Philip's lips despite himself. She was intrepid, he would give her that. "Then present it, by all means," he said, leaning back against the mantle with an air of indifference.

"I intend to," she replied, folding her hands neatly in her lap. "But I will not be insulted in the process. If you have no patience for the truth, perhaps you should excuse yourself."

Emily inhaled sharply, and her mother muttered something about insolence, but Philip found himself intrigued rather than offended. None of the other claimants had shown such spirit.

"You speak brazenly, Miss Letitia," he said briskly. "But bold words do not make you the rightful heiress."

"Nor do they disprove it," she retorted. "The truth will stand, regardless of your doubt."

Aunt Catherine held up a hand, silencing the growing tension. "Enough. We shall examine this claim thoroughly, as we have the others."

As Philip kept his gaze fixed on Letitia, she met his scrutiny without flinching, her composure unshaken. For the first time in months, he felt a trace of uncertainty. Could she truly be the one?

However, as quickly as the thought surfaced, he dismissed it. Beauty and wit were not proof, and he had been deceived before. But he could not deny that he found her spiritedness a refreshing change from the subservient and boring fraudsters. Perhaps she had heard this was the way to get her claim—by pretending to be a member of the nobility and behaving like one. He relished the thought of putting her in her place when the time came. Crossing his arms across his chest, he prepared himself for yet another performance.

The day had just become interesting.

Chapter 3: Letitia

Letitia sat stiffly on the edge of an upholstered chair, her fingers gripping the delicate embroidery of her gown. The dress had been chosen carefully to strike a balance between respectability and humility. She smoothed the fabric nervously as her eyes drifted, almost of their own accord, towards the man standing by the fireplace.

He was the most arrestingly handsome man she had ever seen. Tall and broad-shouldered, he exuded a quiet authority that was as irritating as it was magnetic. His black hair was impeccably combed, and only the amused curve of his mouth softened the sharp angles of his face. Dark blue eyes observed her with a mixture of suspicion and curiosity, their intensity heightened by the glow of the firelight. His tailored coat of deep green superfine fit him perfectly, and his snowy cravat was arranged with such precision that Letitia felt sure he had not a single hair out of place.

But she found him despicable because of the way he had spoken to her and treated them as if they were there to beg for bread. While she understood he might be frustrated with the goings and comings of the women pretending to be her, it did not give him the right to insult and cast her aside before hearing her tale. And that had sharpened her tongue against her better judgment. But he had riled her to the point that she had not been able to keep quiet despite her aunt's silent urgings to remain calm.

"Do you make it a habit to gape at strangers, Miss Letitia?" the duke's voice, smooth and clipped, held an edge of sarcasm.

Letitia flushed, tearing her gaze away as one of the older women in the room—a severe-looking lady with an air of grandeur—snapped, "It is exceedingly rude to stare."

"My apologies," Letitia remarked with embarrassment. She turned her gaze to the floor, her cheeks burning. She hated that she had been caught staring, but he was the most striking man she had ever seen.

But I must not make a cake of myself because of him, particularly as he does not care for my presence here.

Aunt Helen, seated beside her, reached over and gave her hand a reassuring squeeze before addressing the room. "We have not come to impose, but merely to state the truth and to present the rightful heiress to Wynthorpe. Letitia's birth is no fabrication, I assure you."

The severe-looking woman, whom Letitia guessed was the formidable matriarch of the household, raised an eyebrow. "And yet you bring no credible explanation as to why you have waited two decades to appear."

Aunt Helen straightened in her chair, her eyes meeting the older woman's with quiet defiance. "The truth is simple. After my sister passed, I feared for Letitia's safety. The circumstances surrounding her parents' marriage were... delicate."

"Delicate?" she pressed. "Or scandalous?"

Letitia bristled at the censorious tone, but Aunt Helen remained calm. "Call it what you will, madam. Lord Harrowfield married my sister, Clara, in secret. They were deeply in love but bound by the constraints of society. He feared his family would reject her because she was a commoner. When Clara died a few days after giving birth to Letitia, Lord Harrowfield was heartbroken, but he ensured Letitia's safety by entrusting her to me. When I discovered Letitia's life was in danger, I sent word to him. When I did not hear from him, I took her away to ensure her continued survival."

"How terribly noble," the duke drawled. "And yet, that does not explain why you have chosen this precise moment to make yourselves known."

"Because until recently, I believed it was safer for her to stay away," Aunt Helen replied coolly.

The older woman scoffed. "And you just took the child away? It did not cross your mind that my brother would have been looking for you and his daughter, even though he mentioned none of this to me."

Aunt Helen sighed. "I did try to reach him even after we left. I wrote to him three times to explain everything and where we were, but he never replied. So, I took it to mean that he was not interested in having anything to do with his daughter. I thought maybe he still feared for her safety if he were to make public knowledge and acceptance of her. Or he feared she might be rejected, just like her mother."

Letitia swallowed thickly. She had had to come to terms with the knowledge that her late father had set her aside as if she did not exist. Thankfully, she had found a man to call a father to fill the gap.

"Not even after he passed away?" one of the younger ladies asked.

"I did not know of his demise until a long time later."

"Still, you did not come forward until now," the older woman mentioned in an accusatory tone.

Letitia gritted her teeth inwardly. She did not like this line of questioning that was making Aunt Helen look as if she had done something wrong and she was lying.

"When I read of the late duke's passing and the search for his granddaughter, I realized it was safe for Letitia to come and take her rightful place."

The duke exchanged a skeptical glance with the older woman who had been speaking. She pursed her lips. The other elderly woman sitting across from Letitia added her voice to the interrogation. "And where is this proof you claim to have? A mere tale will not suffice, Mrs. Robinson."

Aunt Helen hesitated for the briefest moment before reaching into her reticule. She withdrew a small, weathered portrait encased in a simple wooden frame and some letters and handed them to the duke. "This was painted shortly after their wedding. It depicts Lord and Lady Harrowfield. And they wrote the letters to each other before and after their marriage, some of which my sister never had the chance to send to him before her demise."

The duke took the portrait, his expression unreadable as he studied it. "A pretty painting, to be sure," he said finally, handing it to the older woman, "but hardly conclusive. Anyone could have commissioned it."

Letitia clenched her jaw. "You dismiss it so easily, yet you fail to offer a better explanation for why they would be painted together."

His arresting blue eyes shifted to hers, and a spark of amusement mingled with his suspicion. "I am simply wary of deceit, Miss Letitia. You admitted yourself that this is not the first time someone has arrived claiming to be the duke's granddaughter but is not."

"And perhaps if you did not treat everyone with such disdain, you would not have to deal with so many pretenders," Letitia shot back, sharper than she intended.

The other elderly woman's eyes widened at her impertinence, but his lips twitched as if suppressing a smile. "Touché. Though I doubt your forthrightness will do much to bolster your case."

Letitia drew herself up, her posture as regal as any queen's. "I do not require your approval. I merely request that you give me and my aunt the courtesy of listening to the truth."

Before he could retort, Aunt Helen said, "Read the letters. You will clearly see the marquess wrote them to my sister."

He snorted and passed the papers into the eager hands of the women. Letitia blinked back her tears because she had read and reread the love letters her parents had shared. The beautiful words showed a deep love between a man and a woman who were bound by society but defied it. Again, her heart clenched, for she wished she had known her actual parents.

The matriarch shook her head. "While the handwriting looks like Henry's, we cannot say for certain that it is his. Forgers could easily have written them."

It took everything in Letitia not to snap at the woman. The papers were aged and some of the ink fading, so she could not understand how she could be calling it fake.

Aunt Helen was wrong. We should not have come. These people are not really looking for me. There must be something going on that I do not know about.

She had been so nervous to meet her father's family, but Aunt Helen and Frances had given her the courage to face them. However, the reception they had received so far was hardly welcoming. She almost wished they would declare her a charlatan like the others, so they could return to Brookstone and forget about the entire ordeal.

Aunt Helen pulled a small object from her reticule. It was a delicate gold locket on a fine chain. She placed it gently on the table in front of them. It was the gift she had given to Letitia on her eighteenth birthday—her most prized possession, which she recently discovered had belonged to her mother.

"This belonged to Clara," her aunt whispered. "It was a gift from the marquess on their wedding day. Inside, you will find their engraved initials, and beneath it, the emblem of the Wynthorpe title."

The matriarch reached for the locket, her fingers trembling slightly. She opened it with care, her countenance shifting from scepticism to something closer to astonishment. "This... this looks genuine," she admitted. "It resembles the one that belonged to my mother, given by the first son in the family to their wives. I have not seen it since my mother gave it to my brother before her demise."

The other woman leaned over to examine the locket as well, her eyes narrowing. "Are you sure?"

She nodded and looked away, obviously distressed by the sight of the locket... or possibly a memory of her deceased family.

The duke nodded, his stance rigid despite the murmurs of surprise. "Even if the locket is authentic, it does not prove *she* is the rightful heiress."

Letitia stood abruptly, her eyes blazing. "What more do you require? A signed affidavit from my late father? A séance to summon his spirit?"

"Letitia!" Aunt Helen admonished, pulling her back into her seat.

The duke's lips curved into a faint smile. "Your passion is commendable, though your sarcasm less so."

"I see sarcasm is something you have mastered," Letitia countered.

The tension in the room thickened until the older woman raised a hand. "Enough," she said firmly. "The solicitor must be summoned to authenticate this evidence. Until then, we can draw no conclusions."

He inclined his head. "A sensible course of action. In the meantime, Miss Letitia, I trust you will not take offence if we refrain from celebrating your inheritance just yet."

Letitia shrugged. "Celebrate or not, the truth will remain unchanged."

As he moved to ring for the butler, Letitia allowed herself a brief moment to collect her thoughts. The hostility in the room was palpable, but she refused to be intimidated. She had a mind to leave such an antagonistic environment, but she wanted to relish the look on their faces—especially the duke's—when it was proven that she was indeed the rightful heiress. Surreptitiously, she observed him as he instructed the butler to send a footman to fetch the solicitor posthaste.

Yes, she would take delight in making him squirm and beg for her forgiveness for his unpardonable behavior.

Chapter 4: Philip

This is unbearable!

Philip, standing by the French windows, could not tear his gaze from the small, golden object glinting in the light. His posture was outwardly composed, but inside, tension roiled. The drawing room was quiet, save for the occasional rustle of parchment as Mr. Hadlock, the family solicitor, scrutinized the locket.

The women had taken their seats at the far end of the room. Aunt Catherine sat stiffly, her mien unreadable, while Mrs. Trowbridge whispered something to Emily, her sharp eyes darting occasionally toward the solicitor. Letitia sat beside her aunt, her back straight, her hands folded in her lap. Philip caught himself observing her again, intrigued by the absence of self-satisfaction in her demeanor. If she were another charlatan, she was remarkably convincing... and beautiful.

He ground his teeth, enraged with himself for being unable to ignore her stunning features.

"Well?" Philip could not help snapping with impatience at the older man. He itched to put the new claimant in her place and have her out of his hair as soon as possible. He did not like the way he was reacting to her.

Hadlock finally cleared his throat, drawing the room's attention. He adjusted his spectacles, his brow furrowed as he examined the miniature inside the locket. "This is precisely as described by the late duke. Lord Harrowfield was explicit about its design, particularly the initials engraved here." He tapped the locket lightly. "I can confirm this belonged to Her Grace, Lady Wynthorpe, who gave it to her son, Lord Harrowfield, who in turn gave it to his wife."

Letitia's aunt let out a soft, audible sigh of relief. "Thank you, Mr. Hadlock. At least now, perhaps, you can see I have spoken the truth."

Mrs. Trowbridge looked unconvinced, but Aunt Catherine leaned forward with a stiff face. "And what of Miss Letitia herself? Does she match my late brother's descriptions of his wife?"

Hadlock nodded slowly. "Indeed. Lord Harrowfield spoke fondly of his wife to his father. I believe he mentioned she had dark curls and lovely features. Miss Letitia bears a striking resemblance to those accounts." He glanced toward the portrait Letitia's aunt had presented earlier. "And the painting further supports this claim."

Philip's lips pressed into a thin line. His instincts, honed from dealing with false claimants for weeks, told him this time was different. But he was not ready to concede. "You are certain, then, Mr. Hadlock?"

The older man straightened in the armchair with a solemn look. "I see no reason to doubt it, Your Grace. The locket is authentic, and Mrs. Robinson has shared details about the marquess and her sister that only someone intimately connected to them could know, like the church where they were wed, the clergyman who officiated the ceremony, and the witnesses. Also, the handwriting in the letters and on the marriage register, which we obtained, is similar. I think they have proven beyond reasonable doubt that Miss Letitia is indeed Lord and Lady Harrowfield's missing daughter."

Philip exhaled slowly. "Very well. Thank you. Your assistance is invaluable."

The solicitor nodded, packed up his notes, and took his leave. The tension in the room stayed even after the door closed behind him.

Aunt Catherine, her tone carefully impassive, addressed Letitia. "Welcome to the family, such as it is. I am Catherine, your... your... aunt. My daughter, Maria, is seated here." She gestured to Maria, who offered Letitia a tentative nod. "Mrs. Trowbridge and her daughter, Emily, are dear friends of the family. And, of course, our cousin and the new duke, Philip Henshaw."

Letitia rose and curtsied gracefully. "It is a pleasure to meet you all. I have no great demands, I assure you. I came not for wealth but to know my family, my father's family, that is."

Philip's gaze sharpened at her words. Alarm bells rang in his mind. *They all say that, do they not?*

The last five fraudsters had claimed the same noble intentions, and each time, they had revealed their true colors soon after.

As Letitia took her seat, she deliberately turned to look at him, as if expecting him to say something. He would rather have his tongue cut out than admit he was wrong about her. Even though Hadlock had substantiated her story and the proofs she brought, he was still wary of accepting her at face value. And so he merely ignored her, shifting the direction of his gaze.

After the maid Aunt Catherine had summoned by ringing the small bell on the table appeared to escort Letitia, her aunt, and her cousin to their rooms, Philip remained in the drawing room with the other women.

"I dare say the entire charade has finally come to an end," he mentioned with a small smile.

Aunt Catherine wasted no time to speak in low, urgent tones. "Do you truly believe she is my niece?"

He shrugged. "Hadlock proved it, did he not?"

She waved her hand in disgust. "I am sorry, but I am not wholly convinced."

Even though he shared her sentiment, he sighed with exasperation. "What more do you need? None of the others presented a locket, let alone letters and a portrait."

She sniffed with annoyance. "They are not enough to me. Did you not see how easily she spoke those fake words of family commitment?"

He pinched the bridge of his nose. "But her features clearly show she is a Barrington."

She eyed him with suspicion. "Surely you cannot allow yourself to be taken in by a pretty face."

He stiffened, though he kept his face blank. "I am not so easily swayed by appearances, Aunt Catherine."

"Perhaps not," she said pointedly, "but such beauty has fooled even the shrewdest men. We agreed upon a pact, did we not?"

He groaned inwardly. He had agreed, but now he was not certain he wanted to continue with it. "I see no benefit in proceeding with that plan."

Mrs. Trowbridge frowned. "You cannot abandon it now. The girl may very well be another fraudster, Your Grace. You must test her."

"Test her how?" he questioned with a touch of exasperation. "Hadlock has verified the locket and her story. What more proof do you ladies need?"

Maria, silent until now, spoke up timidly. "Perhaps... perhaps you could find out her true intentions. Tell her you are in dire financial straits, that the estate is struggling, and you need the money urgently."

A frown contorted his forehead. "Do you mean to suggest I feign poverty?"

Emily nodded emphatically. "Yes. 'Tis a brilliant idea. It would be the perfect test. If she is genuine, she will not waver in her desire to help *her family*. But if she is after wealth, she will show her hand."

He let out a soft, humorless laugh. "I am hardly a pauper, Emily. It would strain credibility to pretend otherwise."

"Then say you have debts," Aunt Catherine pressed. "Say the estate is tied up in legal matters. Anything to gauge her reaction."

He rubbed his temples, frustration simmering beneath his composed exterior. How did he find himself in such a quagmire? The title was becoming more troublesome than he had envisaged.

Heaven save me from desperate, manipulative women!

"And if she proves herself? Will you leave her be?"

Aunt Catherine paused, then nodded reluctantly. "If she passes this test, we will not interfere further. We shall accept her wholeheartedly as a part of our family."

He stood abruptly, his chair scraping against the polished floor. He had to leave before they came up with another outrageous plan. "Very well. But do not expect me to enjoy this charade."

Maria's soft voice followed him as he left the room. "You are doing the right thing, Philip. Truly."

He did not respond, striding instead to the sanctuary of the study. The familiar scent of aged leather and tobacco greeted him as he closed the door behind him. He sank into the armchair by the fireplace, staring into the dying embers.

This was not what he had envisioned for his role as duke. Deception and suspicion were hardly fitting for the head of a noble family, but his responsibility was clear. He had to protect the Wynthorpe title and ensure the estate was not taken in by an impostor.

And yet, his thoughts drifted to Letitia—her beauty and her poised responses. She had not seemed elated by Hadlock's confirmation, nor conceited in her victory. If anything, she had appeared indifferent, almost weary. For someone who had spoken brazenly to him earlier, he had expected her to laugh in his face and demand an apology. Her quiet acceptance of Hadlock's proclamation was suspect.

He sighed, raking his fingers through his hair. Had she been surprised by how easily she had fooled them? Was her spiritedness merely an act to throw them off the game she was playing?

What are you hiding, Lady Letitia Barrington? Whatever it was, he would find out.

Chapter 5: Letitia

"This is amazing."

The room was unlike anything Letitia had ever seen. The bed was a grand four-poster with heavy brocade curtains in a soft emerald hue matching the plush carpet that sank beneath her slippered feet. The furniture was mahogany, gleaming under the light of a crystal chandelier. A faint floral scent filled the room from the intricate vase of roses on a side table. The large windows overlooked the manicured gardens below, and sunlight streamed in.

Frances spun in a slow circle, her eyes wide with awe. "Lettie, it is simply splendid! Have you ever imagined such luxury?"

Letitia smiled brightly. "Never! It feels like stepping into another world." She ran her hand over the fine fabric of a chaise longue near the fireplace. "Do you think it is too grand for us?"

Frances laughed softly. "Too grand? Nonsense! It is precisely what you deserve, *Lady Letitia*."

Both of them giggled helplessly.

Aunt Helen's sharp voice cut through their excitement. "Enough of that chatter. You must remember why we are here." She glanced at the closed door behind her and lowered her voice. "Do not forget that they... your father's family are still strangers. I do not think they trust us. Every smile, every gesture could be a ruse. We must tread carefully."

The reminder dampened Letitia's mood. She sank onto the edge of the bed, her fingers gripping the embroidered coverlet. "I noticed their animosity," she admitted. Especially the duke's, but she did not wish to think about him. "I had hoped for... not warmth, but civility at least."

Aunt Helen's face softened slightly. "It will take time, my dear. But until we are certain of our standing, remain cautious. Trust no one."

Frances pouted. "Must you always be so serious, Mama? Can we not enjoy even a moment of this—?"

A knock interrupted her. A maid entered, curtsying neatly. "Lady Letitia, His Grace requests your presence in the study."

Letitia's stomach tightened at the title. Lady Letitia. She did not know if she would ever get used to it. And she was a little surprised that it had already been bestowed upon her. Did that mean her family truly accepted her as the missing granddaughter or, just as her aunt cautioned, was it merely a travesty?

She faltered in her steps, glancing at her aunt for guidance. "Mama?"

"Go," Aunt Helen said firmly. "But be wary of him. The duke is not to be underestimated. Do not trade words with him like you did earlier. Speak carefully and listen even more cautiously."

Letitia smoothed her gown. "Very well, Mama."

The maid led her down the wide, winding staircase, its polished bannisters gleaming in the light spilling through the grand arched windows. The foyer below was an architectural marvel—marble floors in a checkerboard pattern, towering columns, and walls adorned with portraits of stern-looking ancestors. A crystal chandelier hung overhead, glittering.

Letitia halted her steps, her eyes tracing one of the paintings—a man with strikingly familiar eyes and a noble bearing. Her grandfather, she realized. The thought brought both comfort and trepidation. He had tried to have her killed when she was a baby, and now he was the reason she was there. She did not know what to think about him.

The maid stopped at the foot of the stairs while the butler led her to a pair of heavy oak doors. He knocked briefly, then opened one to announce, "Lady Letitia, Your Grace."

Pushing away her nerves, Letitia walked gracefully inside. The study was warm and masculine, with dark wood paneling and shelves filled with leather-bound volumes. The air carried the faint scent of aged parchment and pipe tobacco.

Philip rose from behind a massive mahogany desk. Again, her heart missed a beat at how good-looking he was in his dark waistcoat and impeccably tailored coat, his cravat tied with precision. His height and bearing were regal, and his penetrating blue eyes locked on her with an intensity that made her pulse quicken.

She curtsied, keeping her face expressionless even though he was the most handsome man her eyes had ever beheld. "Your Grace."

"Lady Letitia," he said smoothly, gesturing to a chair opposite him. "Please, be seated."

Letitia's steps were unhurried as she approached and sat. The leather chair was cool beneath her fingertips, and she kept her back straight, unwilling to appear anything but composed.

Philip settled back into his chair, his fingers steepled. "I must apologize for my earlier conduct," he began. "We have had our share of... unscrupulous claimants. It has left us wary."

Letitia's breath caught in her throat. Of all the things she had expected from him, an apology was the least. She inclined her head. "I understand, Your Grace. I would likely feel the same in your position."

His lips quirked, but the gesture did not reach his eyes. "You are gracious. However, I must speak plainly."

She pursed her lips as she braced herself for what he was about to say.

"For the sake of the estate and the family, I would ask you to reconsider your claim."

Her brows knit together. "I beg your pardon?"

He leaned forward, his voice soft but firm. "Return to the countryside, Lady Letitia. Leave this matter behind. The estate will ensure you, your aunt, and her family are provided for—a generous allowance, more than sufficient for a comfortable life."

Her brow furrowed. "Why?"

He sighed. "Because if you do not agree, your aunt, your cousin… and… I will be left destitute. Aunt Catherine and Maria will be left without a home, or a means of sustenance, and I fear that I face debtor's prison due to enormous debts. Surely you must understand that it is not fair that after we have toiled and taken great care of your grandfather, he should bequeath his wealth to you, leaving the rest of his family in penury."

Letitia gawked at him with horror. Now she understood the animosity she had received from them. She felt like a usurper, coming from nowhere to take their means of livelihood. But why would her grandfather be so cruel as to cast aside his family for more or less a stranger? Or was she being strung along? Surely the late duke knew his family better and had reasons for cutting them off. Or was he really as wicked as her aunt had told her?

For a moment, his earnest tone nearly swayed her. But then she caught the faint glimmer of satisfaction in his eyes, a trace of calculation that ignited her anger. She sat back, her gaze narrowing.

He is trying to hoodwink me into giving up my inheritance.

"I see," she said coolly. "You wish to see me gone."

He shook his head. "It is not as simple as that."

"Oh, but it is," she retorted. "You would have me vanish, tucked away neatly in some distant village while you and yours enjoy the fruits of *my* grandfather's labor."

"You misunderstand," he said sharply. "This is not about greed—"

"No? Then why insist I relinquish what is rightfully mine? Have you no honor or sense of duty?"

His jaw tightened. "You have no idea what you speak of. Were you not the one who claimed only a short while ago that you were here to know your family and not for the wealth?"

She blushed. "Yes, but I am inclined to change my mind, given the way you just tried to trick me and the unsavory welcome I received."

He snorted. "Unsavory welcome? You come from nowhere, claiming kinship and wealth—"

"Because it is the truth!" she interrupted, her voice rising. "Or do you still accuse me of fabricating my lineage, despite the locket, despite the portrait, despite everything?"

He stood abruptly, his chair scraping against the floor. "You speak of truth and yet fail to acknowledge the sacrifices made by those who tended to your grandfather in his final years. Where were you then?"

She rose as well, her cheeks flushing. "And where were you when my grandfather was making his fortune? Lurking around to get your greedy hands on it? Shall we say you find inheriting only the title unsatisfactory? Or perhaps we should focus on your current attempt to steal what you clearly feel entitled to?"

His eyes burned with rage, and for a moment, the tension crackling between them felt almost tangible. "You presume much, my lady. You know nothing of me or my sacrifices."

"And you know nothing of me," she shot back, her voice trembling with suppressed fury. "Do not mistake my arrival here as some scheme for wealth. I came to find my family, though it seems I have found only hostility."

Their gazes locked, both defiant, neither willing to yield. The air between them was charged, and Letitia's heart raced—not just from anger, but from something she refused to name.

He snarled. "You will regret this decision."

She lifted her chin. "I shall take my chances, *Your Grace*."

Without waiting for his reply, she turned and strode toward the door, her steps echoing in the silence. Her hand shook as she grasped the handle, but she forced herself to appear unruffled.

The journey back to her room felt endless. The grandeur of the house no longer impressed her; it loomed, cold and unwelcoming. By the time she reached the sanctuary of her chambers, her fury had dimmed, replaced by a strange mixture of unease and exhilaration.

She pressed a hand to her chest, willing her heart to stop thundering. Whatever else might happen, she could not deny the undeniable pull she felt toward the infuriating duke. And that, more than his threats or accusations, frightened her most of all.

Chapter 6: Philip

Philip sat stiffly in the salon, his face set like granite as the minutes ticked by. The sunrays flooding through the tall, mullioned windows dappled the polished wood floor, but its warmth did little to thaw his dark mood. He was supposed to be teaching Letitia how to ride, a task stipulated by the late duke's will—a clause Philip was beginning to suspect was crafted solely to torment him. His great-uncle had specified that the entire family was to make Letitia's transition into society smooth, especially with the Season beginning soon.

God's blood, where is she? I do not have all day to dillydally!

The door creaked open, and a maid appeared, curtsying hastily.

"Lady Letitia will be down shortly, Your Grace."

Philip nodded curtly, drumming his fingers on the carved armrest of his chair. He wished there was a way to get out of the task, but he owed it to the Barrington family to see it through, particularly as Letitia made it known to him three days ago that she would not leave it all behind. His face stiffened at the memory of their encounter in the study. It had taken his brothers' encouraging words to make his way to the townhouse that morning, and now she was late.

Shortly turned into another ten minutes before Letitia finally entered. She wore a simple muslin day dress in pale blue, the high waist cinched with a ribbon, but it was the apple she was noisily chewing that made his mouth tighten.

Lord, give me patience.

"Good heavens," he snapped, rising to his full height, his dark blue frock coat moving with him. "Do you have no sense of decorum?"

Letitia paused mid-bite, the rosy apple still at her lips. "Good morning to you, too, Your Grace," she said with sweet sarcasm.

"'Tis nearly noon," he retorted with impatience. "You are late. 'Tis unbecoming of a lady to be tardy."

She shrugged, taking another bite. "I was not aware we had an appointment."

He drew in a sharp breath. "You received my note yesterday. Do not attempt to deny it."

She blinked at him with wide, feigned innocence. "What note? I received nothing."

Liar. He knew for a fact the butler had delivered it. He had already asked *Forbes* when he realized Letitia was not ready and waiting for him upon his arrival. But he was too exasperated to argue. "You cannot ride in that dress," he said bluntly, his gaze sweeping her attire. The basic cut did nothing to hide the soft curves beneath, nor the porcelain silkiness of her skin, and he forced his mind back to the matter at hand. Registering how beautiful she looked even in the simplest of dresses would do him no good.

"This is all I have," she replied tightly.

"Then we shall have to order a new wardrobe," he said through gritted teeth. "Where is your chaperone?"

"My what?"

He pinched the bridge of his nose. "You cannot gallivant about without one. Fetch a maid—or your cousin."

She tilted her head with rebellion in her emerald eyes. "Frances is sleeping."

"Then wake her," he remarked in a clipped tone.

"But—"

"I shall wait... a little longer."

She stared at him as if debating whether to defy him further before spinning on her heel and leaving. Philip exhaled sharply, pacing the room to keep from throwing something.

Patience, Philip. Remember you are doing this for the Barringtons, not the haughty twit.

By the time Letitia returned with Frances, yawning and rubbing her eyes, his patience was a fraying thread. But he strove hard to control it. He merely spun on his heel and walked away, not waiting to see if they would follow him.

Outside, the spring air was fresh and cool and carried the faint scent of blossoms and newly turned earth. The Wynthorpe stables were a proud structure of red brick and dark timber, their slate roof glinting in the sunlight. Inside, the stalls were immaculately clean, each housing a well-bred horse with sleek coat and intelligent eyes.

Philip gestured towards a chestnut mare. "This is Dahlia," he said in a brisk tone. "She is gentle enough for a beginner."

Letitia drew abreast, stroking the mare's velvety nose. "She is beautiful," she murmured.

"Yes, well, appearances can be deceiving," he muttered, his gaze flicking to her dress again. "I suppose this will have to do for now."

The stable hands saddled the horses while Frances cooed over a placid grey gelding. Philip helped them mount, his strong hands firm as he lifted Letitia onto Dahlia. For a moment, her scent—something light and floral—wafted towards him, distracting him and making him hold on to her some seconds longer as something inexplicable trickled through him.

Curse it!

He hastened away from her, wondering what was wrong with him. With angry steps, he walked to the black stallion. It was not as if he had not seen a beautiful woman before, so he did not understand why this uncultured one affected him so much.

Before he could mount his own horse, the two women nudged their steeds into motion, galloping out of the stable yard with laughter trailing behind them.

"Blasted fools," he grumbled, mounting quickly. "They will break their necks."

The open countryside unfurled before them, green and vibrant under the spring sun. Philip urged his stallion into a gallop, closing the gap between them. Angrily, he realized both young women were not strangers to riding. Why did they not tell him instead of allowing him to waste his time? Perhaps to make a fool of him. He caught up just as Letitia was pulling Dahlia to a halt near a hedgerow.

"What in heaven's name were you thinking?" he barked. "You cannot simply ride off like that!"

Letitia turned to him, her cheeks flushed from the wind. "We were merely having a bit of fun."

"Fun?" he parroted, incredulous. "Do you even understand the word 'etiquette'? Or has your life in the country stripped you of all sense of propriety?"

Her emerald eyes sparkled like embers. "I may be from the country, but I am not some unrefined savage. Perhaps you, with all your airs and arrogance, might consider that not everyone has been spoon-fed rules and decorum since birth."

"Arrogance?" He leaned closer, his blue eyes scorching with fury. "I am attempting to prevent you from disgracing the family name. Wynthorpe is not some backwater estate to be trampled upon by ill-mannered—"

"Pompous louts?" she interjected in a scathing tone. "Because that is precisely what you are. Overbearing, impatient, and utterly incapable of seeing beyond your own inflated ego."

Frances, perched on her horse a few feet away, watched the exchange with wide eyes, her head swiveling back and forth as though at a fencing match.

"You are insufferable," he threw at her with icy rage. "If you think you can waltz into this family and—"

"And what?" she snapped. "Claim what is legally mine? Or is it that you are afraid, Your Grace, that a mere country girl might prove more deserving than you?"

For some reason he could not understand, he found the image of her with eyes blazing and her wind-tousled hair very alluring. And it angered him immensely.

He closed the distance between them abruptly, his tall frame imposing as he approached her horse. "This ends now. You will return to the house and reflect on your unruly behavior. Perhaps then you will understand the weight of what it means to bear the Wynthorpe title."

She glared at him, her chin slanted rebelliously. "And perhaps you should reflect on what it means to be a man of honor, rather than a bully who hides behind his title."

For some seconds, neither spoke, their heated gazes locked. The air thrummed with strain, and something inexplicable passed between them, causing Philip's body to stiffen with awareness.

Then, with a huff, Letitia turned her horse and began the slow ride back to the house, Frances riding beside her.

Philip sat there, his hands clenched on the reins, watching her retreating figure. The field was quiet again, save for the rustle of leaves in the breeze.

What was it about this lady that had him so much on the edge? If only he could renounce the Wynthorpe title and be done with the Barringtons. But he could not let Aunt Catherine and Maria down.

"Darnation!" He was beginning to suspect that Letitia would be the death of him.

Chapter 7: Letitia

For the next two weeks, Letitia found herself caught in a whirlwind of lessons, rules, and endless corrections. The grand hall of the Wynthorpe estate resonated not just with her determined footsteps but with the giggles of Maria and Emily, who seemed to take great delight in her many mishaps.

One morning, Letitia was seated in the grand dining room, the clink of silverware marking the start of yet another meal fraught with unspoken expectations. The table stretched endlessly, laden with crystal glasses and ornate silver serving dishes, but her eyes were fixed on the dizzying array of forks before her.

"You have chosen the wrong one," Maria spoke loudly from across the table, her lips twitching with amusement.

Letitia glanced down at the fork in her hand. It was slightly larger than the others, but seemingly adequate for the task of spearing the delicate asparagus. "It is a fork. It works," she said flippantly, trying to ignore the heat creeping up her neck.

Emily giggled. "That one is for the fish course."

Letitia groaned inwardly. "There is a fork *just for fish*? How many blasted forks does one meal require?"

Maria smirked. "You are not supposed to say 'blasted' either. It is unladylike."

With a frustrated huff, Letitia plucked another fork from the table and jabbed it at her asparagus. The vegetable resisted her efforts, sliding stubbornly across her plate until it toppled over the edge and landed on the pristine white tablecloth.

"Oh, dear," Maria said, her shoulders shaking with laughter.

Emily covered her mouth, her eyes dancing with mirth.

Letitia dropped the offending fork and sat back in her chair, folding her arms. "I will eat nothing but soup from now on. No forks required."

This declaration only prompted louder laughter, which Philip, seated at the far end of the table, did not share. His eyes grazed to Letitia briefly before returning to his plate. His countenance was incomprehensible, but she would not be surprised if he were laughing at her inwardly. Possibly only propriety kept him from mocking her the way the others have been doing.

"'Tis so easy to claim wealth, but not so easy to behave in a way befitting the wealth," Maria whispered fiercely with malice in her eyes.

Letitia blushed and fought not to respond to the taunt. She would do whatever it took to make them all see that she could be a lady befitting her new station.

But the walking lesson proved no better.

"Keep your chin level, Letitia," Aunt Catherine instructed from the edge of the drawing room, her sharp eyes following Letitia's every move. "And for heaven's sake, glide. You are not stomping through a field!"

Letitia attempted another step, balancing a heavy book on her head as instructed. Her gown, a soft lavender sprigged muslin, swished about her ankles as she tried to mimic the elegant movements of Maria and Emily.

"Like this," Emily said, demonstrating an impossibly graceful turn.

Letitia followed, nearly succeeding, but the book wobbled and slid from her head, narrowly missing Maria's foot.

"Goodness, Letitia!" Maria cried, jumping back. "You nearly maimed me!"

Letitia glared at the offending book now lying on the carpet. "Perhaps if I were allowed to walk without balancing half the library on my head, I might have better luck."

Aunt Catherine sighed audibly, and Maria and Emily dissolved into another fit of giggles.

"Perhaps this is just a waste of time and you are not cut out to become a lady," she told her curtly.

The color drained from Letitia's face as the other young ladies smiled with satisfaction.

She was trying her best, yet it seemed as if it was all in vain. She was aware that her relatives had still not warmed up to her, but constantly reminding her that she did not have it in her to become a proper lady was distressing. However, she was determined to make them eat their words.

A week later, Aunt Helen announced her departure for Brookstone to care for her ailing husband. Letitia was saddened by the news because her aunt and Frances had been a supporting pillar throughout her ordeal of becoming a suitable lady. However, she was overjoyed with relief that Frances had decided to stay behind.

"I could not leave you alone with those strangers who do not seem to mean well for you, Lettie," Frances said as they sat in the parlor later that afternoon. "Besides, the entertainment here is far superior to anything in the country."

Letitia gave her a grateful smile. "You are a saint, Fran. I would likely perish from sheer mortification otherwise."

Frances laughed. "Perish you might, but at least you would do so dramatically. Now, shall we review your etiquette lessons again?"

Letitia groaned. "No more forks, I beg of you."

***

The ballroom gleamed with the soft glow of freshly polished floors and gold-plated mirrors reflecting the late afternoon light. Letitia hesitated in the doorway, her heart racing. She was late for her dancing lesson, thanks to the maid providing the wrong time. Again.

Philip stood near the center of the room, his dark hair gleaming, his figure as impeccable as always in a dark green coat and cream-colored waistcoat, and black trousers and shiny shoes. His expression, however, was less welcoming.

"You are late," he said without preamble.

Letitia curtsied stiffly, deciding not to provoke him further since she was in the wrong. "The maid gave me the incorrect time. Again."

His forehead creased in a frown, but he said nothing more. Instead, he held out his hand.

"Let us begin. The waltz is simple enough, provided you pay attention."

Letitia hesitated before placing her gloved hand in his. The warmth of his touch sent an unsettling jolt through her, and she looked away quickly. Her nose wriggled from his intoxicating cedar fragrance. She wished she could hold her breath to keep from inhaling it, but she was certain she would swoon and pass out. And surely, he would see it as an excuse for her not to practice her dance lessons with him. He always thought the worst of her. She could hardly blame him. After all, she had been challenging him from the very first day they met. Given his arrogance, she did not think he was used to being challenged.

He led her into position, his arm firm around her waist as he guided her into the first step. "One, two, three. One, two, three. Do you feel the rhythm?"

"I feel like a klutz," she groused, just before her foot landed squarely on his.

He winced but did not release her. "Relax. You are overthinking it."

"Easy for you to say," she grumbled. "You are not the one stomping about like a cow in clogs."

He arched a brow. "I assure you, Lady Letitia, I have endured worse."

She frowned. "You mean to say I am not the worst student you have had?"

"You are certainly... memorable," he said dryly, a faint smile playing at the corners of his lips.

She flushed, unsure whether to be insulted or flattered. The scent of cedar emanating from him was distracting, and the steady pressure of his hand on her waist made her feel oddly weightless.

Another misstep brought her back to reality. "I am hopeless," she said, stepping away abruptly.

"You are improving," he replied evenly.

"Liar."

"Persistent," he corrected.

She could bear it no longer. The intensity of his presence, his voice, his nearness—it was too much. "I... I... am afraid I... am tired from all these lessons," she blurted, striding further back. "I must rest."

Before he could protest, she curtsied hastily and fled the room.

Frances was waiting for her in the bedchamber, reclining against the pillows with a book and a mischievous grin. "Well? Why are you back so soon? How did your lesson go?"

Letitia collapsed onto the bed, her cheeks still warm. "I am a disaster."

"Nonsense," Frances said cheerfully. "I am sure His Grace would disagree."

"Philip?" Letitia sat up abruptly. "What has he to do with anything?"

Frances arched a brow. "Oh, nothing. Except you are blushing like a rose in bloom, and you fled your lesson as though your hair were on fire."

Letitia groaned, burying her face in her hands. "You are incorrigible."

"And you, my dear cousin, are smitten," Frances teased.

"I most certainly am not!"

"His Grace is *very* handsome," Frances continued, ignoring Letitia's protest. "If I were not a '*commoner*,' I might set my sights on him myself."

"You are speaking nonsense," Letitia said firmly, though her heart betrayed her with a quickened beat. "Why would I be smitten by such an arrogant man who tried to trick me into giving up my inheritance?"

"All I hear are excuses. I have been watching you. No one has ever gotten you riled and flustered the way he does. Methinks there is more to it than you are letting on."

With a flushed cheek, Letitia waved her hand in the air. "Utter balderdash. He takes delight in riling me so I will return to Brookstone. For you to think I have taken a fancy to such a devious fellow is a complete insult to my person."

For an answer, her cousin simply gazed at her with a twinkle in her eyes and giggled. "You two will make a perfect couple, though. The Duke and Duchess of Wynthorpe."

A knock on the door saved Letitia from further torment. A maid entered, curtsying. "It is time for your French lesson, my lady."

Letitia leapt to her feet, eager for an escape. "Thank you."

But when she arrived at the designated room, a crochet needle and yarn awaited her instead of French books.

She groaned aloud. "Someone is determined to drive me mad."

Chapter 8: Philip

The raucous laughter from James and Charles grated on Philip's nerves. White's was far too crowded for his liking that afternoon, but his brothers seemed to thrive on the lively atmosphere. Seated in a corner, their card game was interrupted more by jesting than strategy, much to Philip's growing irritation.

"She stepped on your foot *again* yesterday?" Charles, his youngest brother, smirked, shuffling the deck with deliberate nonchalance. Like Philip's, his dark hair gleamed in the sunlight pouring through the tall windows. "Good Lord, Philip, you may need armor for these lessons. Perhaps steel-toed boots?"

James, his immediate younger brother, snorted into his drink, his blue eyes like Philip's, twinkling with amusement. "You cannot seriously be this aggrieved over a young lady's missteps. She has, after all, spent her entire life in the countryside. What did you expect? A polished debutante?"

Philip's jaw tightened as he threw his cards onto the table in exasperation. "I expected punctuality at the very least," he snapped.

"And perhaps an ounce of humility. But no, Lady Letitia Barrington is tardy, clumsy, undignified, blames everyone else for her failures, and stumbles through her lessons like an untrained filly."

Charles leaned back in his chair, his grin widening. "It sounds to me as though you have met your match, brother."

Philip scowled. "This is no jest, Charles. If she continues in this manner, she will bring disgrace to the Barrington name. Our great-uncle's will be cursed! I cannot make a lady out of someone who refuses to listen."

James exchanged a look with Charles before fixing his older brother with a knowing gaze. "You are too hard on her, Philip. The girl has spent two decades running about in meadows. You cannot expect her to transform overnight."

Philip waved off the sentiment with a dismissive hand. "Enough of making excuses for her. If you were in my shoes, you would not be so understanding. She would try the patience of a saint, I tell you." He sighed audibly. "I have another dancing lesson with her today, and I dread to think what condition my feet will be in by supper." He stood abruptly, pushing back his chair. "If I do not return, assume she has killed me in a fit of pique."

Charles's laughter followed him out the door, much to Philip's chagrin. He should have followed his instincts and relinquished the title to James. He did not think his brother would be this considerate if *he* had to deal with the hellion.

Philip arrived at the Wynthorpe townhouse with his usual precision, stepping out of his carriage into the warm spring air. The scent of blooming flowers mingled with the distant hum of street vendors peddling their wares. Despite the serene beauty of the day, his mood remained sour.

Inside, the grand ballroom shone with polished floors and towering windows that let in a flood of sun rays. Philip stood by the pianoforte, his arms crossed as he waited. And waited.

"She is late again," he muttered to no one in particular. The maid who had been sent to fetch Letitia returned, looking apologetic. As usual.

"Lady Letitia will be down shortly, Your Grace. She said she was misinformed about the time."

He pinched the bridge of his nose. "Of course she was."

Minutes later, the door burst open, and Letitia entered with all the poise of a startled colt. She was clad in a soft blue muslin gown that, while not overly elaborate, flattered her slightly curvy figure in a way that Philip tried very hard not to notice. Her dark curls were disheveled, as though she had hurriedly pinned them in place.

"You are late. Yet again," he mentioned in a clipped voice.

She sighed, brushing an errant curl from her forehead. "It is not my fault, I assure you. The maid told me the wrong hour."

Philip's lips thinned. "How convenient. I suppose the maid also neglected to inform you that punctuality is a hallmark of any respectable lady."

Her eyes darkened with annoyance. "If you have come to lecture me, perhaps we ought to forgo the dancing altogether. I am certain your toes will thank you."

He stared at her for a moment, torn between irritation and amusement. Deciding that arguing would only delay the inevitable, he extended his hand. "Shall we begin?"

She dithered, her bravado faltering as she placed her hand in his. "I apologize in advance if I tread on you. I am not having the best of days."

He suppressed a sigh. "Do not apologize. Simply focus."

He led her to the center of the room, positioning her hand on his shoulder while his own rested lightly on her waist. The moment her fingers brushed against him, warmth spread through his chest, and he swiftly ignored it. As usual. He was getting used to the sensations that flooded him whenever he held her in his arms.

"Now, follow my lead," he instructed.

She nodded, her eyebrows knitted in concentration. At first, their steps were awkward, her foot catching on his every few beats. He winced as her heel collided with his boot for the third time.

"I am sorry!" she exclaimed, looking genuinely distressed.

"Do not apologize," he repeated in a strained voice. "Keep your head up and watch where you place your feet."

She tried again, her movements stiffer now. He sighed, softening his tone. "Relax. Dancing is not a military drill."

"Easy for you to say," she grumbled. "You were likely born waltzing."

A corner of his mouth twitched. "Hardly. My first lessons were disastrous, though I doubt you would believe it."

She glanced up at him, her emerald eyes wide with surprise. "Truly?"

"Truly." He guided her through another turn. "Now, let us try that again. And this time, do not look at your feet."

Their steps began to flow more smoothly, though Letitia's tension did not entirely dissipate. As they danced, Philip found himself acutely aware of her proximity: the light floral scent with a hint of lavender in her hair and the warmth of her hand in his. It was maddening, entirely too pleasant for his comfort.

"You are improving," he said grudgingly.

"Am I?" she asked, a hint of hope in her voice.

He nodded. "Marginally. Though I daresay my toes may never recover."

She laughed a soft, musical sound that caught him off guard. For a moment, he forgot his irritation and stared at her. He took a steadying breath as an unwelcome jolt shot through him. He was becoming too conscious of her beauty and the feel of her in his arms, and it was getting to him.

To distract himself, he cleared his throat. "How are your lessons progressing?" he asked, aiming for casual indifference and hoping she could not hear his thundering heart.

Her eyebrows drew together, and she exhaled loudly. "Progressing? That would imply there is progress."

His lips twitched, almost betraying his amusement, but he remained silent as she launched into an impassioned tirade.

"I was given the wrong time for my French lesson yesterday and arrived just as the tutor was departing. When I asked Mrs. Somerville about it, she said she had written it down correctly, so clearly, someone changed it. Then, this morning, I was told to be in one of the rooms on the first floor for my embroidery lesson, only to find out it had been moved to the east drawing room without anyone informing me." She huffed, a stray curl bouncing near her cheek.

He shook his head. "Do you not think, perhaps, that there might have been some...miscommunication on your part?"

Her eyes brightened with ire. "Miscommunication? How am I to know where to go if I am deliberately misled? Why, even during my etiquette lesson, Maria and Emily kept giggling behind their fans, though I am certain they were the ones who 'accidentally' placed the fish fork in the wrong spot at dinner. Everyone here seems determined to make me look foolish!"

He arched an eyebrow, struggling to suppress the surge of irritation. "Everyone? Or could it be, Lady Letitia, that you are looking for others to blame for your own...shortcomings?"

Her mouth fell open, and annoyance colored her face. "Shortcomings? You think it is my fault? Your Grace, I have done nothing but try to—"

Another sharp step on his foot interrupted her argument. He winced, swallowing the expletive that threatened to escape. "Focus, Lady Letitia," he bit out icily. "This is a waltz, not a march through the marshes."

And then she stepped on him again. And then twice more although she looked as if she was concentrating. When her heel hit his shoe one more time and he saw the glint in her eyes, he realized she was doing it intentionally, probably sulking because he had not accepted her excuses for her failings.

"Cease such childishness, Lady Letitia!" he snapped but she stepped on him again. He released her abruptly and moved back. "I have had enough. You blame everyone but yourself for your failures, and you treat every lesson as though it is some grand inconvenience."

Her face tightened. "And you treat me as though I am some hapless fool incapable of learning. Perhaps if you were not so insufferably pompous, I might actually enjoy these lessons!"

His rage kindled. "Enjoyment has nothing to do with it. If you cannot take this seriously, you will bring disgrace upon yourself and the family. You can dress the part, look the part, and even imitate your betters, *Lady* Letitia, but you *will never* be a lady."

The words hung in the air like a slap. Letitia's face paled, her eyes glistening with unshed tears. Without a word, she turned and fled the room, the sound of her footsteps echoing through the hall.

Philip stood frozen, regret coursing through him. He had gone too far and allowed his frustration to dictate his words. Swearing under his breath, he ran a hand through his hair, wishing for the hundredth time that he could simply walk away from this entire ordeal. But duty bound him, as it always had.

With a heavy sigh, he left the ballroom, vowing to make amends. If only he knew where to begin.

Chapter 9: Letitia

The early afternoon sunlight slanted through the drawing room's expansive windows. Letitia stood stiffly as Aunt Catherine's sharp voice cut through the air like a blade.

"How many times must I tell you, Letitia? A lady does not shirk her lessons! You missed your piano session this morning, and Mrs. Tremaine was kept waiting in vain," Aunt Catherine scolded, her lips thinning as she glared at her niece.

"I did not know she was coming," Letitia said quietly, her hands clasped tightly in front of her.

Aunt Catherine's hand shot up to silence her. "Do not make excuses! You are the most irresponsible, insufferable girl I have ever had the misfortune of meeting!"

"Oh, for heaven's sake! You are *always* claiming ignorance," Maria interjected, her voice dripping with condescension. She was seated on a high-backed chair near the window, dressed in a pale yellow muslin gown that complemented her porcelain skin. "The servants apparently never inform you of anything. How very convenient!"

Emily, resting with elegance on a chaise lounge, snickered. "She must think us fools to believe her incessant lies. Truly, it is not ignorance, it is laziness. Admit it, Letitia. You care naught for refinement. You are only here to inherit your grandfather's fortune and squander it."

Letitia's hands balled into fists. "That is not true."

Emily sat up, her dark green gown swirling around her as she leaned forward, a glint of malice in her eyes. "Oh, but it *is*. Do you think we do not see through you? You may dress yourself in silk and lace, but you will always be a coarse country peasant."

It took everything in Letitia not to retaliate as she stood there while Maria and Emily took turns throwing malicious jabs at her.

"That is enough, Emily," Mrs. Trowbridge said mildly. She sat quietly in the corner, her expression unprejudiced, her needlepoint resting in her lap.

Letitia swallowed hard, fighting the urge to snap back at them because she knew that was what they were expecting; so, they would call her rude, arrogant, and incapable of accepting correction, however unfairly given. She could already feel the tears of indignation stinging her eyes, but she refused to let them fall in front of these women. It would be a victory they would savor.

"I beg your leave," she said, her voice trembling despite her best efforts.

Aunt Catherine waved her hand dismissively, her beaded bracelets jingling. "Go. You are a hopeless case."

The moment Letitia was outside the room, she lifted the skirts of her dress and broke into a run, her silk slippers tapping against the marble floors. Her breathing was shallow, and her chest tight with pent-up frustration. She bypassed the grand staircase that led to the upper floors and headed instead for the garden. She did not wish for

Frances to see her so distressed. Her cousin might ask them to take leave of such horrible relatives, but she was determined to prove them wrong.

The moment she ran outside, the fresh air hit her face. She made her way to the gazebo, tucked away at the far end of the manicured grounds. The gravel path crunched underfoot as she hurried, her skirts swishing around her ankles.

The garden was a masterpiece, a blend of color and scent. Hedges shaped into intricate designs framed flowerbeds bursting with dahlias, roses, and sweet peas. A fountain stood at the center, its clear water cascading gracefully. Birds chirped in the trees, their melodies blending with the gentle hum of bees flitting among the blooms.

The gazebo was painted white, its delicate latticework entwined with climbing ivy. Inside, there were a small round table and a few wrought-iron chairs. Letitia sank onto one of them, the cool metal biting through the fabric of her gown. She buried her face in her hands and sobbed.

Her tears came in great, heaving gasps as she thought of the life she had left behind in Brookstone. The simple cottage, the rolling meadows, and the wildflowers she used to gather. It had been a humble life, but it was peaceful. There were no cutting words, no disdainful glances, no relentless reminders of how she fell short.

Her fingers smoothed over the fabric of her dress. It was a lovely creation—a deep lavender silk adorned with delicate embroidery. It fit her perfectly, thanks to the seamstress Philip had sent to take her measurements. A week later, trunks filled with exquisite gowns, shoes, and accessories had arrived. She should have felt like a princess with such luxury, but she felt like an imposter.

She wished with all her heart that her aunt had not come across the newspaper relaying the information that her grandfather had left her an heiress. Perhaps she should have insisted she wanted no business with the Barringtons. It was sad that she had come in order to know her father's family, but no one would speak to her about the deceased man. It defeated the purpose of coming there in the first place. All they saw in her was an interloper, not a family member.

The sound of footsteps behind her interrupted her thoughts. Her heart sank. Had either Maria or Emily followed her to deliver more barbs? She hastily wiped her tears and turned, bracing herself.

A handkerchief, snow-white and edged with fine embroidery, was thrust into her line of vision.

"Here," came a familiar voice.

Letitia looked up, startled, and her breath caught in her throat.

Philip!

He stood before her, flawlessly attired in a dark red tailcoat and cream-colored breeches, his black cravat tied in an elegant knot. His expression was inscrutable, but his blue eyes—those mesmerizing blue eyes that reminded her of sapphires—betrayed something akin to concern.

She groaned inwardly. Of all people, why *him*?

***

"Come to mock me, have you? Or perhaps to gloat?" she mumbled, brushing her fingers hastily beneath her damp eyes.

His eyebrow furrowed as he drew abreast, the worry in his eyes taking her off guard. "Mock you? Lady Letitia, I will do no such thing. And as for gloating, I am hardly in the mood."

She narrowed her eyes filled with suspicion at him. "I find that very hard to believe. Your family has had a field day at my expense, and you are no different. I have not forgotten so easily our encounter yesterday. Or the cutting remarks you made about my so-called unruly behavior."

He winced at the reminder, his expression one of regret. "I... Yes, I was harsh. Too hard on you." He released a heavy sigh when she stared at him in disbelief. "I overheard what they said just now, and they were wrong—every word. I came here to apologize."

The words left his lips with surprising ease, but Letitia could only gape at him. Philip Henshaw, the Duke of Wynthorpe, apologizing? The man who never missed an opportunity to point out her flaws? She must be hallucinating.

"You...you apologize?" she stammered. "Have you taken ill, Your Grace?"

A smile pulled at his lips, softening the sharpness of his features. "I deserve that," he admitted, crouching slightly to meet her gaze. "And I deserve worse for how I treated you. But believe me when I say I am sorry, Lady Letitia. Truly."

Her lips parted, but no sharp retort came to mind. The genuine sincerity in his eyes rendered her speechless.

Surely I must be dreaming? Or does he have an agenda for apologizing and being gentle with me?

"I know it has not been easy for you," he continued quietly as though speaking too loudly might shatter the fragile moment between them. "Being thrust into this world with so many expectations and so many rules cannot be easy. My family has no excuse for their behavior." He ran a hand through his hair. "And neither do I. You deserve better."

Letitia blinked rapidly, the lump in her throat swelling anew. To her horror, fresh tears pricked at her eyes. She looked away, determined not to let him see her so undone again.

"You cannot mean that," she said testily. "Your family seems to think I am beyond hope. And perhaps they are right."

"They are not right." His tone was firm, and she could not resist glancing at him again. "And if you think I would let them—or anyone—convince you otherwise, you are sorely mistaken."

Her heart stirred at the unexpected warmth in his voice, but she fought to quell the fluttering sensation. "Why are you being so kind to me now?" she demanded calmly.

He paused, his gaze dropping to the handkerchief in his hand before extending it again. "Because... I have seen how hard you are trying. And because I know this life is new to you. It would be unjust of me to fault you for what you cannot yet control. I only came to that realization after our...our altercation yesterday."

Her fingers curled around the handkerchief reluctantly, and she pressed the crisp linen against her skin. She inhaled the faint smell of his cedar scent on the fabric and smiled a little. "I do not know what to say."

"You need not say anything," he replied, straightening. "Though if you wish to scold me further, I am prepared to endure it."

A reluctant smile broke through her defenses, the absurdity of his statement coaxing a laugh from her. "You truly are insufferable, Your Grace."

"Insufferable and charming, I hope," he quipped, his eyes twinkling. "Now, may I sit with you? It is a lovely day, and I find myself unwilling to leave the garden just yet."

She hesitated, wary of his sudden change in demeanor. But the earnestness in his manner swayed her, and she nodded. "If you must."

He settled beside her on the bench, his movements fluid and unhurried. For some minutes, neither spoke, the tranquility of the garden filling the silence. A gentle breeze rustled the ivy that clung to its pillars, carrying the soft whir of insects as they flitted through the air.

"I spent a great deal of time in this garden as a boy," Philip said suddenly with nostalgia. "When we were visiting and I grew tired of lessons or quarreling with my brothers, I would escape here."

Letitia glanced at him, curious despite herself. "I cannot imagine you quarreling with anyone. You seem so... composed."

He chuckled, a low, rich sound that made her stomach twist inexplicably. "Oh, you would be surprised. James and Charles—my younger brothers—could tell you many a tale of my less-than-composed moments. I daresay they enjoyed provoking me."

A small smile curved her lips. "And this garden was your refuge?"

"Indeed." He gestured towards the gazebo. "I would sit there for hours, reading or simply enjoying the peace. Though I must confess, the gardens at Wynthorpe are far grander."

Her curiosity sharpened. "Wynthorpe? The ducal estate?"

"The very one," he confirmed, stretching out slightly. "It is a magnificent place. Rolling hills, sprawling grounds, a grand park, and a library that could rival any in London."

Letitia's eyes widened as her imagination painted vivid pictures of the estate. "It sounds like something out of a fairytale."

He smiled faintly. "It is a place of many memories. Perhaps someday you will see it for yourself."

The suggestion caught her off guard, her pulse quickening. "You would... take me there?"

"Why not?" he answered lightly. "Though you might find it rather dull compared to the excitement of town life."

She shook her head, a wistful look crossing her face. "Dull sounds rather appealing, to be honest."

From there, their conversation flowed with surprising ease, the tension that usually lingered between them dissolving as he described the magnificent estate and the times he visited with his mischievous brothers. Letitia found herself laughing more than she had in weeks. Philip's dry wit was a welcome distraction from her earlier misery.

Unexpectedly, a soft cough interrupted their exchange, and they both turned to see a maid standing nearby, her expression apologetic as she curtsied. "I beg your pardon. Lady Letitia, it is time for your stitching lesson."

Letitia sighed, rising reluctantly. "Let us hope it *is* stitching this time and not something else entirely. These lessons have a habit of changing without my knowledge."

Philip regarded her thoughtfully. "You seem rather resigned to your fate, my lady."

She shrugged, smoothing her skirts. "It is easier than fighting it, I suppose."

His smile deepened as he rose. "You continue to surprise me, Lady Letitia. I shall look forward to our next encounter."

The butterflies returned, fluttering madly in her stomach as she curtsied. "Until then, Your Grace."

As she walked away, her heart raced, and she could not help but glance back over her shoulder. Philip was still there, watching her with an unreadable expression.

"Heaven help me withstand such charm" she muttered, her cheeks burning as she hurried away.

Chapter 10: Philip

Philip lingered in the garden, the cool afternoon breeze brushing his face as he stared at the roses. His thoughts were in turmoil.

The memory of Letitia's tears haunted him, and his chest tightened at the recollection of her sobbing distressingly. She had always displayed such strength, such fire, that seeing her in that vulnerable moment had shaken him more than he cared to admit. It had taken everything in him not to draw her in his arms and murmur soothing words. Fear of rejection for all the hurt he had caused her thus far had stopped him. He had thought her incapable of breaking. Her resilience had seemed unshakeable, her spirit fiery even in the face of relentless hostility. The sight of her crumbling under the weight of unkind words had ignited something protective inside him—a feeling he could no longer deny or dismiss.

He inclined forward on the wrought-iron bench, clasping his hand. "You are a fool, Philip," he whispered.

For days, he had tried to convince himself that his growing fondness for Letitia was no more than pity or perhaps duty exacerbated by hiding his feelings under the facade of anger. Yet, the beauty of her face, her spiritedness, and the wit she wielded so effortlessly had unraveled him.

The guilt of his own actions taunted him. He had spoken quite callously to her the day before. How had he let himself be so cruel to someone who had been thrust, unprepared, into their world? And so, he had hurried there to apologize to her after a meeting with his business partners only to hear his family speaking harshly to her. She had not seen him when she ran past him into the garden with tears running down her face. It had touched him to hear her broken sobs. Right there, he had decided to finally adhere to his brothers' words that it cannot be easy for her to be thrust into what she was not accustomed to. He resolved then to change his approach, to honor not only his great-uncle's wishes but the burgeoning respect he felt for her.

With a weary sigh, he rose. As he walked back into the house, he pondered what she had said about her lessons being mixed up. He wondered if someone was intentionally making her look inept. He would not put it past Maria. She barely hid her animosity towards her cousin.

He strode into the drawing room and saw Aunt Catherine seated on the settee, embroidery hoop in hand.

"Philip," she greeted warmly, though her smile faltered when she noticed the solemn expression on his face. "You look as though you carry the weight of the world on your shoulders."

"Good afternoon, Aunt Catherine. I wish to speak with you about Letitia," he said without preamble.

The sharp narrowing of her eyes was almost imperceptible, but Philip caught it. "Letitia? What about her?" she asked curiously, setting aside her embroidery.

"I overheard the conversation you had with her earlier. The way you spoke to her was... unwarranted."

Aunt Catherine's lips pressed into a thin line. "So, she complained to you?"

"She did not," he replied tersely. "I arrived shortly before she fled into the garden. She did not even know I was there. I could not help but hear what was said and be witness to what should never have transpired."

Her face creased in a frown. "You presume to chastise me, Philip? For speaking plainly to a girl who—"

"Who has done nothing to deserve such treatment," he interrupted. "I understand your grievances, Aunt Catherine. The will was unexpected, and its terms—harsh and unjust. But Letitia cannot be blamed for the decisions of her late grandfather."

She arched her eyebrow. "And you have taken it upon yourself to defend her honor?"

"It is not about defending her," he said, his tone sharpening. "It is about treating her with the respect she deserves. Whatever grievances you may have with your father's decisions, they are not her fault."

Her eyes darkened with anger. "Respect? For a girl who has usurped everything that rightfully belongs to you and us?"

He shook his head. "Letitia has usurped nothing. She is the rightful heiress, as confirmed by the will."

"And you are content to accept that?" she questioned, rising abruptly. "Content to watch a stranger take what should have been yours? What kind of a man are you, Philip?"

He met her glare with one of his own. "The kind of man who honors a dead man's wishes, regardless of how unfair they may seem."

She let out a bitter laugh. "Honor? Do not delude yourself. You are defending her because she has bewitched you. It is typical of a man to lose his senses in the presence of a beautiful woman."

Philip bristled. "That is not the case."

"Then what is it?" she demanded. "Why do you defend her so fiercely when she has done nothing but disrupt this family?"

He took a deep breath, willing himself to remain calm. "Because it is the right thing to do. Letitia did not choose this. She did not ask for your resentment, nor has she done anything to deserve it. She has been thrust into a world she barely understands, and instead of offering guidance, we have treated her with disdain."

"And you think she belongs here?" she enquired, her voice quivering with anger. "She is an interloper, Philip. She does not belong here, and she never will." She released a heavy sigh. "Can you not see that she is an outsider thrust into our lives, claiming what should have been yours—what should have remained in the family?"

"That is unfair. She is no trespasser. The evidence is irrefutable—"

"Evidence!" she retorted furiously. "You mean to tell me that because she has emerald eyes and that pendant, we must simply roll over and accept her?" She eyed him with suspicion. "You support her so gallantly, Philip. One might think she has enchanted you with her beauty."

He stiffened. "This is not about enchantment. As I said, it is about honor. You know as well as I that we are bound to respect your late father's demands."

"Do not speak to me of honor, Philip. Where was honor when your inheritance was stolen? When a stranger stepped into a role that should have been yours?"

He grimaced, tired of her acrimony over an innocent girl. "This is not her fault. She did not ask for any of this."

"Did she not?" Her voice dripped with disdain. "Perhaps she is more cunning than I think. Mark my words, Philip, this girl is not what she seems."

"Enough!" he said firmly. "I have no interest in baseless accusations. Letitia is innocent, and I will not stand by while she is treated as a pariah."

She stared at him, her eyes glinting with anger and disbelief. "You are a fool, Philip. Stupid to let her manipulate you. She has taken everything from you, yet you defend her as though she were—" She broke off, her lips constricting into a thin line.

"As though she were what?" he asked, his voice quieter now but no less intense. "Family? That is what she is, Aunt Catherine. Whether or not you accept it."

Her shoulders stiffened, and her hands clenched at her sides. "She will never be family to me," she countered coldly. "She does not belong here. And I will prove it. I will show you that she is nothing more than an opportunist with a pretty face."

He sighed. "Dear Aunt, you gain nothing from such animosity."

She shook her head, frustration clear in every line of her face. "What my father did was unjust, and I will not stand for it."

"Then what would you have me do?" he questioned with exasperation, his voice rising slightly. He was tired of the unproductive conversation. "Turn my back on her? Ignore my conscience and your father's stipulations?"

"Yes!" she cried. "Because she is not one of us. Because she has taken everything from us. Honor our pact since you claim to be a man of honor."

He shook his head. "I cannot do that."

Her eyes shone with fury. "Then you are no better than she is. But hear ye, I shall prove that she is a fraudster like the others!"

With that, she stormed out of the room, leaving Philip alone with his troubled thoughts. He sank onto the settee, raking a hand through his hair. How did it come to this? His family, whom he had always trusted, now seemed consumed by bitterness and resentment. And Letitia... Letitia, who had shown such courage and grace despite everything, was paying the price for her grandfather's decisions.

He sighed deeply, the burden of his predicament weighing on him. He was at a crossroads, torn between loyalty to his family and the growing affection he felt for the woman they all seemed to despise. Letitia was a stranger, yes, but she was not undeserving of kindness. And the more time he spent with her, the harder it became to see her as anything other than remarkable.

How could he reconcile the two? And who should he take sides with?

The stranger he was developing feelings for, or his cousins who were mistreated by his great-uncle?

Chapter 11: Letitia

Letitia stood before the wood-framed mirror in her bedchamber, her hands clasped tightly together to still their trembling. Her emerald silk gown, tailored to perfection, hugged her slender waist before flowing out into a graceful skirt that brushed the floor. Delicate needlepoint of gold threads traced lovely patterns along the bodice and hem, shimmering like sunlight on water. The short sleeves rested just off her shoulders, revealing her collarbone, where a simple yet elegant emerald pendant rested.

Her gloves, white and elbow-length, were smooth against her creamy skin, and her satin slippers peeked out from beneath the hem of her gown, their pointed toes adorned with tiny sparkling emerald buckles. Her hair, styled in soft curls, was swept into a stylish chignon, with a few tendrils framing her face. Dainty hairpins of emeralds and diamonds sparkled in her dark locks, completing her transformation from a country girl to a lady fit for a ball—her first ball as Lady Letitia Barrington.

Frances clapped her hands together, a broad smile lighting her face. "Oh, Lettie, you are simply radiant! The color is a perfect match for your eyes. All the gentlemen will be struck dumb the moment they lay eyes on you."

Letitia offered a nervous laugh, adjusting the pendant at her neck. "Do you truly think so? I feel as though I might faint before I even make it to the ballroom."

"Nonsense," Frances said firmly, drawing closer to adjust a stray curl. "You have nothing to fear. Besides, you have His Grace to escort you. He would cut down anyone who dared look at you the wrong way."

A smile lifted Letitia's face and chased away her nervousness for the moment. Philip would indeed champion her cause. He had indeed been kindness itself ever since he found her sobbing in the garden a fortnight ago. Again, her heart fluttered at the thought of him.

A sharp knock at the door interrupted her musing, and a maid entered with a curtsey. "My lady, His Grace awaits you in the foyer."

Letitia's breath rose sharply, but she managed a nod. "Thank you." She reached for her reticule, the gold embellishment glinting in the fading light, and took a steadying breath. "How do I look?"

"Like a vision," Frances said with a dazzling smile. "Now go. You must not keep His Grace waiting."

"I wish you could come with me," she said with a wistful sigh.

"And steal all the attention from you?" Frances teased. "You know I am more beautiful than you. At the mere sight of me, everyone would forget your existence."

As it was meant to achieve, Letitia burst into laughter and drew her cousin into a tight embrace before she exited the room.

Letitia descended the grand staircase with careful steps, her gloved hand trailing lightly along the polished banister. The murmur of voices and the faint scent of fresh flowers from the foyer below reached her as she rounded the last curve.

Philip stood at the bottom of the stairs, his head tilted slightly as he looked up at her. His eyes widened imperceptibly, and a glimmer of something warm crossed his face; something that made her heart leap. He was immaculately clothed in a deep burgundy tailcoat that accentuated his broad shoulders and trim waist. A cream waistcoat embroidered with gold paisley patterns added a touch of elegance, and his white cravat was tied in a perfect waterfall knot against his snowy white shirt. His black trousers fell smoothly over his polished Hessian boots, and his hair was neatly combed back, revealing his sharp, angular handsome features.

He extended a hand to her as she reached the bottom step. "Lady Letitia, I am honored to escort the most beautiful lady in all of England tonight."

Her cheeks flushed, and she took his hand. The touch of his warm fingers through her glove sent a pleasant shiver up her arm. "Thank you, Your Grace. You flatter me too much."

"Not at all," he said smoothly, his gaze protracted on hers for a moment longer than propriety dictated. He picked up a velvet wrap from a nearby footman and draped it around her shoulders, his fingers brushing lightly against her arm. She inhaled quietly, the scent of his subtle cologne—a mix of cedar and something faintly spicy—adding to her breathlessness.

The ride to the ball in his opulent ducal carriage was quiet, save for the clatter of the wheels. Philip broke the silence first. "Are you nervous?"

Letitia offered him a small smile and nodded. "A little. This is all so new to me. What if I forget my manners? Or say the wrong thing? Or step on my dance partner's toes? Well, that is if I get any dance offers."

He chuckled. "You will do just fine. Trust me, my lady. Your charm is entirely natural, and you are far more capable than you give yourself credit for. Please do not fret. You have worked hard these weeks past and deserve to enjoy yourself tonight."

His words soothed her, and by the time they arrived at the grand townhouse hosting the evening's festivities, her nerves had settled—though only slightly. The ballroom was already brimming with people, the hum of conversation and strains of music spilling out into the vestibule.

Philip took her hand as they waited to be announced. The butler's voice rang out clearly above the din when it was their turn.

"His Grace, the Duke of Wynthorpe, and Lady Letitia Barrington."

All heads turned as they descended the grand staircase, the sea of faces a blur to Letitia as the chandeliers overhead dazzled her. The ladies were bedecked in vibrant silks and satins, their jewels sparkling, while the gentlemen's tailored coats and starched cravats completed the brilliant display of refinement.

"Smile, my lady," Philip whispered near her ear, his breath warm against her cheek.

"Everyone is staring. 'Tis all so overwhelming," she whispered back, hoping she would not tumble down the stairs in her nervousness.

Why so many steps? She grumbled inwardly.

He chuckled. "That is because you have been the subject of speculation all this while and the *ton* did not expect you to be so beautiful. You are meant to enjoy the attention, as I am right now because I am the envy of all the men present."

She giggled.

"Now, picture them as mere ants."

She bit back a laugh and found it easier to relax as people approached them, eager to meet the mysterious Barrington heiress.

Though their names and titles blurred together in her mind, she answered their questions politely and smiled graciously. A few ladies cast envious glances her way, their whispers barely veiled behind their fans, but Letitia refused to let them rattle her.

Philip's brothers soon joined them, their resemblance to him unmistakable. Each claimed a dance. James was broad and serious, his kind blue eyes putting her at ease. Charles was rakish and quick with a jest, making her laugh as they took a turn about the room.

But it was Philip who held her attention. Their dance was magnificent, his hand steady at her waist and his movements effortlessly graceful. He teased her with witty remarks about how well she now danced and how happy his feet were, eliciting her laughter even as she struggled to remember the steps.

"Careful, my lady," he murmured with a mischievous smile. "You will have the gentlemen lining up to propose if you keep laughing like that."

"Only if they wish to trip over my feet," she replied, grinning.

Laughter rumbled from his throat. "Given the manner in which they have been ogling you all evening, I dare say they would not mind."

Letitia had to acknowledge that she had received a lot of attention from the men. Her dance card was full, and the men who were not on it had grimaced with disappointment when she told them. She wondered if it was the enigma of her being unknown or if it was because of her supposed wealth. Not once did it cross her mind that it was because she was a stunningly beautiful lady.

When the dance ended, Philip excused himself to fetch her a glass of punch. Letitia waited near the edge of the room, her heart light and her spirits high. She had not expected to enjoy herself so thoroughly. Philip was right. Her introduction into society was a success.

But her happiness dimmed as Maria approached, her expression cold. Letitia wondered what she wanted. After all, she, her mother, and Emily had ignored her all this while. It grated on her nerves that they had shown all of London that they were not in support of her. However, Letitia straightened, offering a polite smile.

"Maria," she said cautiously. "What a lovely evening this has been."

"For you, perhaps," Maria replied icily before taking a sip from her cup. Her eyes flicked over Letitia's gown. "I must admit, you are quite the spectacle tonight. A great hit with everyone, it seems."

Letitia frowned, unsure how to respond. Before she could say anything, Maria's hand moved sharply, and the contents of her punch cup splashed across Letitia's emerald gown.

"Oh, how clumsy of me," Maria said with mock concern, her lips curling into a smug smile.

Letitia's breath caught as the sticky liquid seeped into the fabric, the humiliation of the moment sinking in as she stared at the spreading stain.

***

The indistinct murmur of curious whispers followed Letitia as she fled the ballroom, her emerald skirts swishing with each hurried step. The scent of orange blossoms and candle wax grew fainter the further she moved from the grandeur of the ballroom, replaced by the cool stillness of the corridor. Her pulse thudded painfully in her ears as she reached the retiring room, pushing the door open and shutting it firmly behind her.

Inside, the room was modest but elegant, with framed mirrors adorning the walls and a chaise lounge in the corner. She caught sight of herself in one of the mirrors. Her gown, which had been pristine and magnificent mere moments ago, was now marred by an unsightly dark stain near her hip. Anger surged within her as she thought of Maria's smug expression. She had the mind of repaying her cousin in kind, but she knew that was exactly what the witch wanted. Maria sought to ruin her splendid night, but she would not let her.

"May I assist you, my lady?" The voice of a maid startled her from her thoughts. The young woman curtsied and gestured towards a basin of water.

"Yes, please," Letitia said with relief. "If it is not too much trouble."

The maid worked quickly, using a cloth and some powdered chalk to dab at the spill. "It will not be perfect, my lady, but it shall be much improved."

Letitia watched as the stain gradually faded, her ire simmering just beneath the surface. "Thank you. You have been most helpful."

The maid offered a warm smile. "You look beautiful, my lady. The ballroom would be lesser without you."

Letitia's lips twitched in a faint smile. "That is kind of you to say."

After ensuring her gown was presentable once more, she left the retiring room. The corridor was quiet save for the soft thrum of distant voices, and as she turned a corner, she found herself face-to-face with Philip.

He straightened from where he had been leaning against the wall. Once more, her pulse raced at the sight of his handsome visage. His eyes studied her with concern. "Are you all right, my lady?"

For a moment, she considered telling him everything—the venom in Maria's tone, and the deliberate malice in her actions—but she hesitated. What if he took Maria's side as he had before?

"I am fine," she said, forcing a small smile. "I simply needed a moment."

He did not look convinced but did not press her. "If you do not wish to return to the ballroom just yet, may I suggest the garden? It is far quieter."

Relieved by his understanding, she nodded. "That would be lovely."

He offered her his arm, and they strolled together through the hallways until they reached the doors leading to the garden. Outside, the cool night air was a welcome reprieve from the heat of the ballroom. Lanterns hung along the paths, throwing a golden glow over the hedgerows and flowerbeds. Groups of people loitered here and there, some smoking cigars, others engaged in soft conversation.

Philip guided her to a secluded stone bench beneath a trellis of ivy. "It is a fine evening," he remarked, taking a seat beside her.

"It is indeed," she replied, smoothing her skirts. His proximity was unnervingly distracting.

They began talking, first of inconsequential matters—the weather, the festivities, the peculiarities of certain guests—but their conversation soon deepened.

"Tell me about your childhood," he demanded, slanting his head as he observed her. "Did you enjoy the countryside, or did you yearn for the city?"

She laughed softly. "The countryside was my solace. I often spent hours roaming the fields and woods near the village. My mother... I beg your pardon, my aunt who I thought was my mother, found it most unbecoming."

"I can hardly imagine you as anything but becoming," he remarked lightly.

Heat rose to her cheeks. "And you? Were you always so... proper?"

He chuckled. "Far from it. My brothers and I were a menace. My mother despaired of ever raising gentlemen."

"I find that difficult to believe," she said, smiling despite herself.

"Then I have deceived you most thoroughly," he teased, his voice lowering as he leaned closer.

Her breath hitched as their fingers brushed against each other on the bench. The accidental touch sent a spark of awareness through her, and she quickly looked away, focusing instead on a cluster of blooming roses nearby.

He reached up and gently tucked a wayward strand of her hair back into her chignon. The contact was brief, but the sensation stayed with her. "There," he said softly. "Perfect once more."

Letitia's heart fluttered in a most unladylike fashion.

Sweet Mary, I am falling for him!

She realized it with startling clarity—but her aunt's warnings echoed in her mind, cautioning her against misplaced trust.

This will not do at all! I have to keep a level head where he is concerned.

"I suppose we ought to return," Philip said, though he made no move to rise.

She found herself reluctant to agree. "Must we? The garden is far more pleasant than the ballroom."

His lips curved in a faint smile. "True, but you would deprive the guests of your lovely company and beauty? It would be a most selfish act."

She laughed, shaking her head. "Very well. Let us return."

Back in the ballroom, the throb of conversation and the strains of the orchestra greeted them. The moment they stepped inside, a handsome gentleman approached her to claim his promised dance. Though Letitia would have preferred to remain by Philip's side, she could hardly refuse.

As she danced, she caught sight of Philip on the far side of the room. He was partnered with an exquisite woman, her auburn hair shining in the candlelight. The sight sent an unexpected pang of jealousy through her chest.

Something is dreadfully wrong with me. I cannot be jealous. Philip is not courting me, so why should this strange desire of wanting to walk over there and yank the lady from his arms plague me?

When the dance ended, her partner escorted her back to where Philip had been standing, only to find Emily waiting for her.

The earl excused himself, and Emily wasted no time. "You should keep your distance from Philip," she said bitingly. "It would be most unwise to form any... attachments."

Letitia frowned, and then the color drained from her face. Was it obvious to all and sundry that she had taken a fancy to the handsome duke?

Biting on her bottom lip and hoping she was wrong, she said, "I do not understand what you mean."

"Do you not?" Emily's smile was frigid. "Philip and I are to be betrothed soon. We are only waiting for my birthday to make the announcement. Surely, you did not think his attentions were genuine?"

Shock rippled through Letitia, rendering her momentarily speechless.

Emily leaned closer, her voice lowering. "He only seeks your fortune, my dear. Did you think his sudden kindness was anything but calculated? A pity you refused to relinquish your wealth outright when he asked you to. Perhaps he believes his devilish charm might achieve what demands could not."

Letitia's heart plunged as Emily's words sank in. Was that why Philip had been so attentive and kind of late?

"Do not look so pale, my dear. I merely seek to warn you because I do not wish to see you make a cake of yourself over him, the handsome devil. Although I would have loved nothing more than to see you brought to shame when our betrothal is announced, I am not in support of him trying to sweeten you to get your money. Yes, we both expected to live a lavish lifestyle with the duke's wealth, but we love each other and that is all that matters to me."

Letitia would have loved nothing more than to call Emily a cruel liar but for her words about Philip demanding she give up her wealth and her refusal to. How did she come about that knowledge if Philip had not told her? It meant they shared confidences about her.

Oh, I have been a fool! A pea-brained, silly girl!

With a gracious smile that belied her turmoil, Letitia replied, "Thank you for the... warning, Emily."

She slipped away before Philip could return, finding a footman and quietly instructing him to fetch Philip's carriage. As she climbed inside, she pressed a hand to her trembling lips, berating herself for being so naive.

"I should have listened to Aunt Helen," she whispered, blinking back tears. But thank goodness she had not worn her heart on her sleeve for him. Now, she would avoid him at all costs.

Chapter 12: Philip

"Curse it!"

Philip stood in the grand entrance hall of the Barringtons' London townhouse, tapping his gloved fingers against his thigh with increasing impatience. Mr. Forbes, with a stoic expression that seemed carved in stone, returned at last.

"Your Grace, Lady Letitia regrets to inform you that she is unavailable to see you today. She also sends her apologies for missing her scheduled lesson."

Philip's forehead creased. "Unavailable? Again?"

The butler inclined his head. "Indeed, Your Grace."

Before Philip could voice his displeasure, the older man bowed and hurriedly walked down the corridor as if he were being chased, leaving him alone in the cavernous place. Philip's hands balled into fists at the audacity, but there was no point taking out his frustration and anger on the messenger. He exhaled sharply and strode to the ballroom, his boots clicking against the polished floor.

He stared at the elegant room where they had spent countless hours practicing for the duchess's ball. The memory of Letitia laughing as he had clumsily attempted a particularly complex turn ran through his mind, and a pang of longing tightened his chest.

What had happened to that ease between them? Ever since the night of the ball, she had been distant, evading him at every turn. She had left without even saying goodbye, instructing the coachman to relay that she had had a sudden blinding headache. He had believed it at the time, but now...

He began pacing the length of the ballroom, his frustration growing with every step. Had he unwittingly offended her? Had someone said something? His mind circled back to their moment in the garden—the quiet companionship, the way her cheeks had flushed under the moonlight, and the way her lips had curved when she had smiled at him. It had felt real, untainted by the artifice of society.

Yet, now she was avoiding him, and he had no idea why.

Unable to stay still, he strode out into the gardens. His boots crunched against the gravel path as he walked past manicured hedges and neatly trimmed flowerbeds.

He stopped near the stone bench where they had sat that afternoon, his fingers brushing the cold, rough surface. He smiled faintly, the memory of her hilarity warming him despite the cool air.

The sound of approaching footsteps broke through his thoughts, and he spun, his heart lifting. "Lady Letitia—"

But it was not Letitia. Emily stood before him, a parasol draped over her arm. She was dressed in a pale lavender walking gown trimmed with lace, her blonde hair perfectly coiffed. She offered him a coy smile, her eyes glinting with something he could not quite place.

"Philip," she said sweetly. "You seem deep in thought."

Philip's polite smile did not quite reach his eyes. "I was hoping to find Letitia. Have you seen her? She has been... elusive as of late."

Emily's lips curved into a knowing smile. "Ah, so you have noticed. She has been rather occupied."

"Occupied?" His eyebrows wrinkled.

"Yes, she has accepted the courtship of a gentleman. Did you not know?"

Philip froze, the words hitting him like a blow. "A gentleman? That is impossible."

Emily raised a delicate brow. "It is not only possible but true. She has been spending a great deal of time with the Earl of Huntington. In fact, they are quite taken with each other. It is why she has been... unavailable to you and nearly everyone else since the morning after her coming-out ball."

A bitter taste filled Philip's mouth. The idea of Letitia courting someone else did not sit well with him. He refused to believe it. However, he composed himself to hide the tumult going on inside him.

"Forgive me, but that seems... unlikely," he said stiffly. "I know her introduction to the peers of the realm was a great success and she had many admirers that night, but Huntington did not approach me on her behalf."

Emily's expression turned sympathetic, though her tone was anything but. "Oh, Philip. If you do not believe me, perhaps you should see for yourself."

He frowned.

"She is at the park with the earl as we speak."

His frown thickened. "But Forbes told me she is unavailable to see me."

She nodded. "That is true. She gave him that excuse just before Lord Huntington came calling and they went to the park. Would you like me to show you?"

Philip wavered, but the temptation to confirm—or refute—Emily's claim was too strong. He gave a curt nod. "Very well."

Together, they climbed into his carriage and rode to the park. Hyde Park, sprawling and vibrant with its winding paths, was busy with the carriages and promenaders of the *ton*.

Philip and Emily walked through the park, the sound of their steps blending with the laughter of children playing nearby and the distant murmur of society's chatter. The greenery was lush, the trees swaying gently in the breeze. Ladies in pastel gowns strolled arm-in-arm with their escorts, and gentlemen in tall hats gathered in clusters, discussing the latest political scandal or racing odds.

"There," Emily said, her voice low but triumphant.

Philip followed the direction of her gaze and saw Letitia.

It cannot be!

She was walking along a gravel path, her hand resting lightly on the arm of a tall, distinguished-looking man. The Earl of Huntington! The earl was impeccably dressed in a dark green coat that complemented his fair hair.

Letitia herself looked radiant in her blue walking gown, which was a perfect match for her delicate features. Her bonnet framed her face, and her soft laughter reached Philip even from a distance. He did not miss the fact that other men at the park were throwing admiring looks her way. However, the sight of her smiling at another man sent a sharp stab of jealousy through him.

He clenched his fists at his sides. Was this why she had been avoiding him? Was this why she had been absent from their lessons, their conversations, and everything else?

As if sensing his gaze, Letitia turned her head slightly. Her eyes met his for a fleeting moment, and something shimmered across her face. Surprise, perhaps, or guilt. But then she looked away, her smile returning as she focused on her companion.

Philip stiffened, feeling as if he had been slapped by her blatant snobbery. He considered approaching her and demanding an explanation, but the presence of Emily at his side and the public setting restrained him. He would not create a scene, not here, no matter how much he would love to rearrange the earl's smiling face.

"Do you believe me now?" Emily asked with a voice dripping with satisfaction.

"Thank you, Emily," he replied tersely. "Your assistance is no longer required."

Without waiting for her response, he turned and strode away, emotions warring within him. Anger, hurt, and something dangerously close to anguish stirred in his chest.

By the time he returned to his townhouse after spending the entire day playing card games and gambling in White's to distract himself from the chaos in his heart, the day had darkened into night. Sleep did not come easily with his mind replaying the scene at the park over and over. He could not reconcile the Letitia he had shared camaraderie in the garden—the one who had laughed and blushed and looked at him with something akin to admiration—with the Letitia he had seen walking so serenely with another man.

What did I do to her to deserve this? Did she sense my growing feelings for her and decide to act this way?

Foolishly, he realized he was the only one who had felt the intense chemistry between them, which was why he had suggested they go back to the ballroom. He had feared that any moment longer with her, he would have drawn her in his arms and kissed her the way he wanted to, not caring if it caused a scandal.

Perhaps if he had told her he was becoming quite fond of her, she would not have seen the need to accept another man's courtship. But would she have believed him? Would she not think he was only after her inheritance?

With a pang, he regretted being a pawn in the hands of Aunt Catherine and Maria. He should never have agreed to ask her to forego her wealth for all their sakes. He had thought he was doing the right thing to allay the fears of his family, but now he understood it was a grievous mistake.

The following morning, he rose early, determined to set things straight. If Letitia would not come to him, then he would go to her. He needed answers, and he would have them, no matter the cost to his pride.

Mounting his horse, he rode through the streets of London, the clatter of hooves on cobblestones mimicking his racing heart. He knew Letitia often rode in the mornings, and it did not take long for him to spot her in the park, her chestnut mare trotting gracefully along the path. Thankfully, there were very few people about.

"Lady Letitia!" he called.

She turned, her posture becoming rigid when she recognized him. Pulling her horse to a halt, she regarded him warily.

Philip wasted no time with pleasantries when he reached her. "You have been avoiding me, my lady. I demand to know why."

Letitia's lips parted, but no words came.

"And while we are at it," he carried on with barely restrained anger, "perhaps you might enlighten me as to the nature of your relationship with the gentleman I saw you with yesterday."

A glint of something crossed her face before she schooled it into a mask of composure.

Please do not say you are already in love with the earl. Please do not tell me you have accepted his offer of marriage.

Philip waited, his heart pounding as he braced himself for her answer.

Chapter 13: Letitia

The cool morning air brushed against Letitia's cheeks as she stared at Philip. She had ridden to the park to clear her head after the tumult of emotions that had plagued her since the day before. She had barely slept after seeing Philip with Emily, her stomach twisting with feelings she dared not name. *How could she be so foolish to think she stood a chance with him?* she had kept asking herself. Of course, Emily suited him better. She was refined, graceful, and, most importantly, part of his circle, even though she was not titled.

Letitia straightened her shoulders, adjusting her grip on the reins as she glared at him. Why was he here? And asking her questions with accusation in his eyes. No, she would not allow him to make her feel guilty for accepting another man's advances. She would focus on herself and her transition into society as a proper lady. She did not need him to guide her anymore. He had served his purpose, and she would not allow herself to be used.

"I am waiting, Lady Letitia."

She forced herself to meet his gaze, tilting her chin up defiantly.

"What are you doing here, Your Grace?" she asked, keeping her tone aloof.

He drew abreast, the early sunlight catching the chiseled lines of his face. "That does not answer my question. Though I suppose it is fortuitous, for I have been meaning to speak with you."

She kept her posture erect. "If it is about my dance lessons, you may rest assured I have no further need of them."

His forehead creased, and his lips thinned. "No further need? Is that so?"

She nodded curtly. "Indeed. I did not step on anyone's toes that night. And I have progressed into society well enough without your help. I daresay I can manage on my own now."

His gaze darkened. "Is that what this is about? Managing on your own? Or is it about avoiding me?"

Before Letitia could reply, her horse startled violently, rearing back and making her grip the reins tautly with fright. A sudden hiss drew her attention to the ground. A snake slithered across the path.

The next moments were obscure to Letitia. Before she could calm the horse, it bolted, and her grip on the reins slipped.

"Philip!" she cried, panic lacing her voice as the animal galloped away uncontrollably.

"Hold on!" Philip shouted.

He spurred his horse forward to catch up. The wind tore through Letitia's bonnet ribbons as her panicked screams filled the air. Just as she thought she might be thrown, a firm hand seized the reins, tugging them firmly. Philip maneuvered his horse alongside hers, pulling both animals to a halt.

Breathless and trembling, Letitia clung to the saddle as Philip drew her horse to a stop. His eyes, taut with concern, searched her face.

"Are you hurt?"

She shook her head, unable to speak at first, shaken by the incident. Although she and Frances enjoyed riding wildly, she had never before experienced a frenzied horse. She willed her thundering heart to slow down.

"Letitia, please talk to me. Are you all right?"

She noticed irrelevantly that he had called her by her name for the first time without the usual title. Against her better judgment, the worry in his voice gave her warmth. Finally, she managed, "Yes, thanks to you."

His mouth curved into a slight smile. "And yet, you claim you no longer need me."

Her cheeks reddened, and she averted her gaze. "You merely happened to be present. It does not mean I require your assistance."

He chuckled, his eyes glinting with amusement. "Ah, I see. This is gratitude in its most elusive form."

She pursed her lips, determined not to be drawn into his teasing. "I meant what I said."

Unexpectedly, the teasing left his eyes, and he turned serious. "Then tell me, my lady, who was that man I saw you with yesterday?"

Her spine stiffened, and she thrust her chin out insolently. "That is none of your concern."

"None of my concern?" His tone hardened. "You are in my care. It is my duty to ensure some opportunistic rogue seeking your fortune does not mislead you."

Like you?

She bit on her tongue to keep from saying it. But before she could stop herself, she snapped, "Then perhaps you should look to your own affairs. I am certain your betrothed would appreciate your attention more than I do."

He blinked, his eyebrow furrowing in confusion. "What? My betrothed? What nonsense are you spouting now?"

"Do not play coy," she retorted. "Emily made it quite clear at the ball that night. *You* are to marry *her*."

A look of surprise crossed his face before he burst into laughter. "Marry Emily? Good heavens, my lady, whatever gave you that idea?"

"Do not laugh at me!" she exclaimed. "She said as much herself."

He shook his head, his amusement fading. "Emily is like a sister to me. There is no truth to what you claim. You must not have heard right, or she must have been jesting."

Letitia's temper flared. "Jesting? Do you take me for a fool? Or is it that you cannot admit the truth about your romantic inclination towards her because she is not an heiress, unlike me?"

He jerked his head as if she had stuck him, and his voice dropped to a dangerous level. "How dare you insinuate such a thing?"

Suddenly, a heated argument ensued between them, neither willing to back down. Frustrated and almost at the brink of tears, Letitia gathered her reins, preparing to ride off.

"Lady Letitia, wait," Philip called. He reached out, catching the reins of her horse.

"Let me go," she demanded tersely, evading his gaze.

"I should not have raised my voice. Forgive me."

Her heart pounded as she elevated her eyes to his.

"I was... jealous," he admitted.

She frowned. "Jealous? Of what?"

He pinched the bridge of his nose before saying, "You are the only woman I have ever known to challenge me so. And, to the best of my knowledge, I am the only man you have known and leaned on since you arrived in London. To avoid me so entirely, only to be seen with another... It stung more than I care to admit."

Letitia's lips parted, the words she wanted to say tangled in her mind. She wanted to tell him the truth about Emily's meddling but held her tongue. Emily had encouraged her to accept the earl's invitation to visit the park so she would not have the reputation of being rude and elusive, having rejected visits from male admirers all week after the ball. She should have known not to listen to Emily. She should have been suspicious about her sudden kindness towards her. But if she told Philip, they would start arguing again, and she was already exhausted. Besides, if he did not believe her before, why would he now?

She opened her mouth to say something, but nothing came out, so she clamped it shut. What could she say about his jealousy? Was he toying with her feelings, or were they real? Could she really believe Emily, who had been cruel to her before the ball, about Philip only being interested in her because of her money?

I am so confused!

"Shall we call a truce, then?" he asked, offering her a tentative smile.

Reluctantly, she nodded. She would have to be very watchful. "Very well."

They spent the rest of the ride in relative peace. Yet, as they returned to the townhouse, Letitia's heart felt heavier than ever.

Philip's kindness, his teasing, his very presence—it all felt too much, too dangerous. How could she trust a man who might only value her for her dowry?

As he helped her dismount at the stables, she resolved to steel her heart. Whatever feelings she harbored for him, she would bury them deep where they could not harm her.

Chapter 14: Philip

*L*etitia Barrington!

Philip reclined back in the high-backed leather chair in his study, the faint scent of aged books and polished wood surrounding him. He stared at the deep mahogany shelves lined with volumes of history and philosophy. But for once, he had little interest in the wisdom of Cicero or the strategies of Caesar.

A smile curved his lips as his mind wandered to the previous evening. The theatre had been splendid. The actors performing *The School for Scandal* had delivered a lively and biting satire of society. But the memory most poignant was Letitia's sharp wit during their heated debate over the play's themes.

"You cannot possibly believe Lady Teazle was in the wrong!" she had exclaimed, her emerald eyes shining with indignation, her fan snapping shut for emphasis.

"And why not?" he had countered, a grin teasing the corners of his mouth. "She married for wealth and position, knowing full well the restrictions such a union would bring. Her frivolity nearly ruined her husband!"

"Frivolity?" Letitia had gasped, looking as though he had insulted her personally. "Lady Teazle was merely reclaiming a piece of herself! If anyone is to blame, it is Sir Peter for failing to understand his wife."

He had laughed then, more delighted than he had any right to be. "Reclaiming herself by courting scandal? Pray, let me never fall afoul of your reasoning, my lady. You would flay me alive with such logic."

She had smirked, her cheeks faintly rosy. "Only if you deserved it."

Now, as he stared out the window at the manicured gardens beyond, he realized he could not recall the last time he had so thoroughly enjoyed a lady's company. Most of the women he encountered were well-mannered to the point of monotony, their conversations limited to trifling compliments or insipid remarks about the weather. Letitia was... different.

"Thinking about her again, are you?"

Philip started, glancing towards the door. James strolled into the study, a knowing smirk on his face. He was dressed casually for the morning, his waistcoat slightly unbuttoned, as though he had only just emerged from a late breakfast.

"I beg your pardon?" Philip said, attempting a casual tone, though he knew the color rising to his cheeks betrayed him.

James chuckled, dropping into the chair opposite. "Spare me your pretense. You are smiling like a schoolboy who has just discovered sugar plums. I would wager my estate that the beautiful Lady Letitia is the cause."

Philip sighed, rubbing the back of his neck. "I do not deny it."

James's eyebrows rose. "Well, that is a first. You, Philip Henshaw, Duke of Wynthorpe, admitting to harboring feelings for a lady? I never thought I would see the day."

Philip shot him a warning look, but it lacked its usual bite. "Do not make me regret my honesty."

"Never," James said, though his grin remained teasing. "But tell me, what do you intend to do about it?"

Philip leaned forward, resting his elbows on the desk. "That is the problem. Letitia is an heiress. If I were to declare my intentions, she might think I am after her fortune."

James's amusement faded, replaced by a frown. "Then tell her the truth. You are a wealthy man in your own right. Her fortune is irrelevant to you."

Philip grimaced. "It is not so simple. I may have... given her the impression that I am not well-off, thanks to Aunt Catherine."

James gave him a look filled with stupefaction. "Why on earth would you do such a thing?"

"It seemed... necessary at the time," Philip admitted in a rueful tone.

James clicked his tongue. "Well, you had best rectify that perception before it comes back to bite you."

Philip knew it was already too late. He had been trying to find the right words to tell Letitia the truth, but for the first time in his life, he did not know how to go about handling the matter. They had declared a truce after her outlandish notion that he harbored romantic feelings for Emily, and he wanted nothing to ruin it as it had been going well and she had declined Lord Huntington's further invitations for her company as well as others. When he confronted Emily about her mischievous ways, she had denied it vehemently, even shedding tears that made him wonder what Letitia had actually heard. He had known Emily all his life and had never seen a trace of guile, so he did not understand what was going on. Maria, the impish hen-wit, must have certainly had a hand in it.

Determined to discover the truth, he said to his brother, "I shall see to it promptly."

He rang the small bell on the table. His butler entered, bowing slightly. Philip rose, straightening his waistcoat. "Inform Abington to prepare the carriage."

"Good for you, old chap," James said brightly. "Mayhap congratulations will be in order when you return."

Philip frowned. "For what?"

James grinned. "For your imminent nuptials."

Philip merely chuckled. "We shall see, James."

He could not tell Letitia the truth about his finances until he found out why she ever thought he would marry Emily. He would force Maria to tell him the truth. Not once did it cross his mind that Letitia might have fabricated the entire story.

***

Philip stepped into the entry hall of the Barringtons' townhouse, his boots clicking sharply against the marble floor as he headed for the sewing room where Forbes had told him he could find Maria.

Arriving there, he was about to thrust open the door when he heard voices. He had not intended to eavesdrop, but the venom he heard in Aunt Catherine's voice caused him to stay his hand.

"Letitia will grow weary soon enough," she said with disdain. "We must simply continue to make her life as unpleasant as possible."

"And if she does not leave?" Maria's voice was petulant. "She is far more stubborn than I expected. I would have bolted back to her inconsequential village were I in her shoes."

"Then we shall escalate matters," her mother replied coldly. "No lady of breeding will endure constant humiliation for long. She will flee back to the countryside where she belongs."

Good Lord!

Philip's blood boiled with ire. Without waiting for further elaboration, he stormed into the room, his eyes blazing.

"Aunt Catherine. Maria."

The two women whirled around, their expressions shifting from surprise to guilt and then to feigned innocence.

"How dare you?" he barked, and Maria jumped.

"Philip, dearest, we were merely—" Aunt Catherine began, but he silenced her with a raised hand.

"Spare me your excuses," he countered heatedly. "I heard everything. You are no longer welcome in this house. Take your scheming elsewhere."

Maria gasped. "You have no right to do that."

His gaze hardened. "I have every right as the Duke of Wynthorpe and the overseer of the Wynthorpes' properties. Letitia is under my protection, and I will not tolerate your scheming."

Aunt Catherine's eyes turned icy. "Surely, you jest. You cannot simply cast us out."

"Watch me," he rejoined tersely. "To think I took sides with you and made her feel she was the one at fault. Whereas *you* were the ones sabotaging her efforts at every turn."

"She deserved whatever we did to her. She does not belong here," the older woman protested.

"Neither do either of you for your cruelty to the true owner of the residence."

"Philip, please." Aunt Catherine took a step forward, but he raised a hand to stop her.

"You will vacate this residence before nightfall. If you cannot show Letitia the respect and love she deserves, then you have no place here. You can only stay or return when you accept her as a legitimate member of the family."

"Philip—"

He cut her off. "For the first time, I understand why your father did what he did. Perhaps he got firsthand knowledge of how cruel you both are, and that was why he wished to leave you nothing."

"How dare you!" she snapped.

"I dare because I have finally seen through you. I was willing to go above and beyond to help and support you, but I draw the line at deliberate cruelty."

A tense silence descended in the room.

Maria glared at him. "You will regret this, Philip."

"I will take my chances," he replied frostily.

The two women swept past him, their skirts rustling angrily as they left the room.

As the door slammed shut behind them, Philip sank into a chair, his head in his hands. Guilt nibbled at him. How many times had he blamed Letitia for imagined slights, believing his aunt's and cousin's lies? He had been blind to their machinations, and Letitia had borne the brunt of it.

He sat there for a long moment, contemplating the damage he had done. But regret alone would not suffice. He would make it up to Letitia, no matter what it took.

He owed her that much and more. He realized with a sting that he owed her even more than he was ready to admit.

Chapter 15: Letitia

Frances sat by the dressing table, carefully untangling a strand of pearls, while Letitia reclined in an armchair, leafing through a book with little attention to its contents. The words blurred as her mind wandered to the previous night at the theatre. The memory of their argument, jesting, and laughter brought a smile to her lips. She had never before seen Philip so relaxed, and they had had such a wonderful time; she had not wanted the evening to end.

Sweet Mary, I am supposed to be staying away from him, but I find that he occupies my thoughts every minute of the day, and when I am in his presence I am breathless. I never knew love could be so encompassing. Poor Andrew, I finally understand how he felt.

"Lettie, are you even reading that book, or are you simply admiring the paper?" Frances teased, glancing up from her task.

Letitia smiled faintly. "It seems my mind refuses to obey me this morning."

Frances giggled. "Dare I say it has something to do with a dashing duke? The reason you have rejected the numerous suitors vying for your hand?"

A blush rose in Letitia's cheeks. "Oh, Fran, how can I hide it from you? Philip has captured my heart."

Before her cousin could reply, the door flew open with such force that the hinges groaned in protest. Aunt Catherine swept in, her skirts billowing as though propelled by a storm. Her face, usually composed into a mask of cold hauteur, was rosy with rage.

"You scheming little minx!" she spat, pointing a trembling finger at Letitia.

Letitia rose, startled. "I beg your pardon?"

"Do not play coy with me!" Aunt Catherine seethed. "You have used your feminine wiles to turn Philip against his own family. How dare you? You have had us sent away like common criminals!"

Letitia's face contorted in confusion. "Sent away? What on earth are you talking about?"

"Do not feign innocence," the older woman countered. "Philip has ordered Maria and me to leave the residence, and we all know it is because of *you*. You may think you have won, but mark my words, Letitia, you will not get away with this."

Before Letitia could respond, the matriarch spun on her heel and stormed out, her footsteps echoing down the corridor.

Letitia stared at the open door, utterly bewildered. "Fran, did I just imagine that?"

Frances, still clutching the strand of pearls, looked equally shocked. "It seems *you* are to blame for their departure, though how remains a mystery. His Grace ordered them to leave?"

"So it would seem," Letitia murmured, sinking back into her chair. "But why would he do such a thing?"

As they exchanged puzzled looks, a knock came at the door, brisk and impatient. Maria entered without waiting for an invitation.

"I suppose you think yourself triumphant," she threw at her cousin with unconcealed bitterness.

Letitia's patience, already worn thin by Aunt Catherine's tirade, began to chafe. "If you have come to cast more accusations, Maria, you will find me ill-prepared to entertain them."

Maria scoffed. "Do not trust him."

"Trust whom?"

"Philip, of course." Maria snapped. "He is no better than the rest of us. Do you honestly believe he is smitten with you? He sent us packing not out of some sense of justice, but because he wants your fortune all for himself. It was always the plan. My mother and I merely underestimated his ambition."

Letitia's heart squeezed in her chest, though she veiled her unease with a calm exterior. She was tired of everyone telling her that the man she had taken a fancy to was a fortune hunter. "That is a grave accusation, Maria."

Maria walked closer. "Believe what you will, but do not say I did not warn you. He is not to be trusted."

With that, Maria removed herself, leaving the room heavy with tension.

Frances exhaled slowly. "Do you think she spoke the truth?"

Letitia shook her head. "I do not know what to think anymore. Emily practically said the same at the ball that night." She raised frantic eyes to her cousin. "What if they are right, Fran? What if Philip is indeed a charlatan, charming me into falling in love with him?"

Frances stood and drew to her side. "Lettie, please do not fall for the ploy of those spiteful witches. He has shown you kindness, where they exhibited cruelty towards you. Surely that is worth more than her malicious words?"

"Perhaps," Letitia murmured. "But he was not always like that if you remember."

"Yes, but you told me he changed when he saw you crying. Perhaps your tears got to him and made him realize how unfair he had been to you."

Letitia chewed on her bottom lip as she contemplated her best friend's words. But Aunt Helen's counsel came back to her. She had to be careful in giving her heart to a man who might indeed only be after her inheritance.

Curse this inheritance! If not for it, I would know Philip's true intentions.

She went to see the only woman who had been kind to her since she arrived at the house, and who also knew Philip well enough.

Mrs. Trowbridge, seated in her modest yet cozy bedchamber, welcomed Letitia with a warm smile. The older woman's presence had always been a source of comfort amidst the chaos of the household.

"What brings you here, my dear?" Mrs. Trowbridge asked, gesturing for Letitia to sit beside her.

"You must have heard that Aunt Catherine and Maria are to leave the residence."

The kindly woman simply nodded and let out a sigh.

"They seem to believe I am the cause. Worse, Maria claims Philip is using me for my fortune."

Mrs. Trowbridge's compassionate eyes softened. "Pay no mind to Maria. She spoke out of jealousy. She and her mother have lost their hold over Philip, and it wounds their pride."

"But what if she is right?"

"She is not," Mrs. Trowbridge said firmly. "Philip may be guarded, but he is not deceitful. If he harbors affection for you, it is because of who you are, not what you possess. Do not let their venom cloud your heart."

Gratitude bloomed inside Letitia as she reached for the older woman's hand. "Thank you."

"Go to him," Mrs. Trowbridge urged with a smile. "I suspect you will find the answers you seek."

Happily, Letitia left the room and hurriedly descended the stairs. She did not know what she would tell Philip, but she wanted to know why he had sent her aunt and cousin packing. The butler told her the duke was in the study.

Letitia entered the room with cautious hope, her heart pounding in her chest after she knocked softly. Her gaze fell upon Philip, who stood near the window. He was not alone.

Emily was in his arms, her head resting against his shoulder as though seeking solace. A warm smile was splashed across Philip's face.

A sharp ache pierced Letitia's chest. She turned on her heel and fled, the hem of her muslin gown sweeping through the corridor as she made her way to the garden.

"Letitia!"

The brittle air stung her cheeks as she stepped onto the gravel path, her breath visible in the cold from the rain that had fallen earlier. She walked briskly, her thoughts a tangled mess of confusion and pain.

"Letitia!"

Philip called out, and she quickened her pace, unwilling to face him. But he caught up, his hand gently clasping her arm to halt her retreat.

"Letitia, please," he said with urgency. "Let me explain."

"There is nothing to explain," she said, refusing to look at him. "Emily is indeed to become your affianced, not just a *friend*. I saw the proof."

"You misunderstood what you saw," he stated strongly. "Emily was upset, and I was comforting her."

Letitia turned to him, her eyes glistening with unshed tears. "Do you expect me to believe that?"

"Yes, because it is the truth. I just made it clear to her that we will never be more than friends. She was hurt, and I did not wish to be cruel."

Letitia searched his face, finding no hint of guile. "Why should I believe you?"

He took a step closer, gazing at her with intense eyes as he cupped her cheek. "Because I love you, Letitia."

Her breath caught in her throat, the words both shocking and exhilarating.

"I never thought I would say those words to any woman," he continued. "But then you came into my life, and everything changed. From just one look at you that day, I was lost forever. I fought hard, not wanting to succumb to the emotion. That was one of the reasons I was always curt with you, as I later realized. It is not only your beauty that took me by storm. I love your spiritedness, your wit, and your courage... I love the way you challenge me and make me laugh. You are unlike any woman I have ever known."

Her lips trembled as she fought to keep her composure. "You forgot to mention my wealth. That you also love my bequeathed fortune."

His face became rigid, and he let out a low sigh. For a moment, he seemed on the verge of saying something. Then he shook his head. "I do not need your money, Letitia. I am content with what I have. You have every reason to doubt me, given the unfortunate thing I said to you that day in the study, which I will eternally regret, but I swear on my late parents' grave that I love you for you, not for your riches."

Can this be true? Dare I believe it? Her heart wanted to, but the seed of doubt Emily and Maria had sown bore fruit inside her.

She moved away from him and his hand fell from her face. She ignored the wariness in his eyes and asked, "Why did you send Aunt Catherine and Maria away?"

He groaned and raked his finger through his dark tresses. "I had hoped to spare you the knowledge, but I reckon you deserve to know."

Her curiosity increased at his words.

"I sent them away because I overheard them plotting to sabotage you further," he admitted.

Her eyes enlarged like dinner plates. "What?"

He nodded. "Yes. They were behind your supposed tardiness and missed lessons and only God knows what else. I could not stand by and let them hurt you any longer."

He covered the short distance between them to take her hands and stare into her eyes. Her mouth ran dry at the fierce emotion she saw in his own blue depths. "I was wrong to believe them and not you. I am sorry for all the times I gave you a hard time when you did not deserve it.

"Henceforth, I promise to always take your side, because I love you, Letitia. And I will let no one hurt you again."

Her head cautioned her to be careful, but her heart refused to listen. Smiling through her tears, she stepped into his arms, clasping him.

"At least one good thing has come out of this," she whispered, smiling like a ninny.

He pulled back to gaze at her with love. "What is it, my darling?"

"You have stopped calling me *Lady Letitia*."

He threw back his head and laughter burst from his throat. "Dare I hope *Your Grace* will become a thing of the past?"

She nodded, smiling shyly.

He kissed her hands and then cupped her cheek. "Would it be too much to ask to hear my name spoken from your sweet lips?"

Her smile widened. "Philip."

"Oh, my darling." He drew her into his arms again.

Letitia clung to him, beaming from ear to ear. All her dreams had come true.

Chapter 16: Philip

A light breeze carried the sweet aroma of lavender, mingling with the faint crunch of leaves from the towering oak trees. Under the shade of one such tree, Philip sat on a plaid blanket, his eyes fixed on Letitia, who sat across from him, her bonnet resting beside her.

She was radiant in her pale green muslin gown, the subtle lace frill around the neckline accentuating the soft blush of her cheeks. Her black hair was arranged in a loose chignon, with a few stray curls framing her beautiful face. A parasol lay discarded at her side, and her gloved hands delicately arranged slices of cake on porcelain plates.

Philip smiled to himself, reveling in the simple perfection of the moment. It had been a week since he confessed his love to her in the garden, and though she had not yet said the words back, he could see the affection in her every glance and gesture. For him, that was enough.

"What has you grinning like a Cheshire cat?" Letitia enquired with a playful smile.

Philip chuckled, reclining back on his elbows. "Is it a crime to be content, my beauty? I am merely enjoying the company of the most enchanting lady in England."

Her cheeks turned a deeper shade of pink, and she averted her eyes. "You are incorrigible, Philip. Truly."

"Only because you inspire it, my love," he replied smoothly, sitting up. "And might I add, you grow lovelier with each passing day."

"You flatter me excessively," she said, though her smile betrayed her pleasure. "But I demand to know what you were truly thinking of."

He reached for a bunch of grapes. "I was recalling the past week, and how beautiful it has been with you by my side. The musicale, the ball, the promenade in the park... Wherever we went, people could not help but remark on how well-matched we are."

Her laugh was soft, almost shy. "Your brothers might disagree, considering how much they seem to enjoy teasing you."

"Ah, yes," Philip said with mock solemnity, "the trials of elder brothers. But I shall endure their taunts, for it is a small price to pay for the privilege of courting you."

She busied herself with rearranging a plate of sandwiches, her blush deepening.

"Letitia, I would like to know more about you. That is, if you do not mind."

She shrugged. "I do not mind. What would you like to know?"

"Your childhood, for instance. I want to know more about it because it aches my heart to know that you grew up without the luxuries that were your due. What was it really like?"

She smiled. "It was simple but happy. We didn't have much—that is, my aunt, whom I believed to be my mother, along with her husband, Frances, and her two brothers, Daniel and Thomas—but we were content. We kept hens, goats, sheep, and a cow for their eggs, meat, and milk, respectively. Papa... eh... my aunt's husband is a blacksmith. Daniel and Thomas helped him at his shop and also worked for Lord Bannerman, who owns the horses that Frances and I enjoyed riding. Aunt Helen is a housekeeper in Lord Bannerman's household while Frances and I worked as scullery maids."

His heart wrenched at the image of her scrubbing pots in the kitchen when she should have been lying in her bed in the Wynthorpe estate, having servants waiting on her.

Perhaps she saw the anguish on his face, for she smiled brightly with nostalgia and said, "Life was unpretentious and beautiful, and I loved it."

More than this one? He yearned to ask, but he already knew his answer as Aunt Catherine and Maria had not treated her well since her arrival.

"Were there any suitors?" he enquired, keeping his tone light, though a slice of jealousy stirred within him.

"Of course," she answered with a laugh. "I am a girl, after all. But none caught my fancy."

"And why is that?" he pushed, observing her intently.

She slanted her head in thought. "Perhaps I am too particular. Or perhaps I simply never felt inclined to marry anyone. I always believed there must be more to marriage than mere convenience."

Her words sent a wave of relief through him, though he masked it with a teasing smile. "Then I count myself fortunate to have won your acceptance of my courtship."

Again, a blush crept up her cheeks, and she looked away. "And what about you? Why have you not married? You could have had your pick of the ladies in London, given the way they bat their eyelids and swoon whenever you are within proximity."

He grinned. "For the same reason as you. I had not fallen in love." His voice softened. "Until now."

Her blush deepened with a vengeance, and she lowered her eyes. "You do have a talent for making me blush like a silly little girl."

"It is a talent I intend to hone," he replied with a smirk. "And do not be envious of the attention I receive from other ladies. It is of no consequence to me."

She raised an eyebrow with a twinkle in her eyes. "Envious? I think not. Merely curious."

"Curious, indeed," he said with a low chuckle. "But let me assure you, they only fawn over me because I am a duke. Just as men are drawn to you for your beauty and fortune."

She laughed. "A thing of the past, now that you are courting me."

He smiled but could not suppress the trace of irritation at the thought of the attention she received wherever they went. Men sought her, even with him by her side. He resolved to ignore it, focusing instead on the joy of being in her company.

As the afternoon wore on, they strolled through the gardens with Frances acting as Letitia's chaperone. The conversation was light and filled with laughter, and Philip could not remember a time when he felt so at ease.

Later that evening, Philip escorted Letitia to the theatre, the event one of the highlights of the social calendar. She was resplendent in a sapphire silk gown decked with silver embroidery, with her hair styled in an elegant twist. The sight of her drew admiring glances from every corner, and Philip could not help but feel a swell of pride... and annoyance at the men ogling her.

The performance that evening was a production of Romeo and Juliet, the tragic romance as captivating as ever. The actors brought the tale to life with passion and poignancy, their voices resonating through the grand theatre.

As the curtains fell on the last act, Philip turned to Letitia. "A masterful performance, do you not agree?"

"Indeed," she replied, smiling. "Though I cannot help but feel that Juliet's choices were rather imprudent. Surely she could have sought counsel from someone more reliable than Friar Laurence?"

Philip laughed. "Ever the practical one, my lady. Perhaps that is why you are no Juliet—you possess far more sense."

"And you, sir, are no Romeo," she responded with a giggle. "For which I am grateful. His impulsiveness would drive me to distraction."

"I shall take that as a compliment," he riposted with a grin. "And may I add, I find your wit as enchanting as your beauty."

Her face reddened, and she looked away. Philip laughed as joy rose in his chest. Indeed, Letitia was everything he ever wanted in a woman. She was beautiful, intelligent, and held his interest as there was never a boring moment with her. A small frown creased his forehead as he thought of asking her to marry him soon because he could not bear to be away from her whenever they parted company, but he feared she might not accept. Possibly, she might say it was too soon as they had not known each other for long. He would have to bide his time.

After escorting Letitia back to her residence and bidding her goodnight, Philip returned to his own home. As he handed his coat, hat, and gloves to his butler, he was informed that a note awaited him in his study. Curious, he strode to the room and broke the wax seal on the envelope. The handwriting was familiar. It was from the private investigator he had employed months ago to look into Letitia's background.

Philip's eyes scanned the paper, and his face darkened with each word.

Your Grace, I am sorry to inform you that Lady Letitia is not the heiress. I have solid proof.

Chapter 17: Letitia

Letitia woke up with a bright smile as the sun's rays spilled through the curtains. As she sat at her dressing table while her cousin helped her brush her hair, the events of the previous day played in her mind. The picnic, the theatre, Philip's smiles—everything seemed like a dream. She was dressed in a soft morning gown of powder blue silk, embroidered with white flowers.

"You are positively glowing this morning, Lettie," Frances mentioned, her eyes glinting with mischief. "Dare I say it is His Grace who has brought such joy to your countenance?"

A flush rose to Letitia's face. "And what if it is?" she replied lightly.

"Do not deny it, Lettie. You are utterly smitten. Is he to propose soon, do you think?"

"I cannot say for certain, Fran," she proclaimed, trying to suppress the smile curving her lips. "But he... he is everything I could wish for in a man and more."

Frances laughed and clapped her hands with glee. "You shall become the future Duchess of Wynthorpe, then."

Their camaraderie was interrupted by the arrival of a maid. "Lady Letitia," the maid said, dipping a curtsy, "you are summoned to the drawing room."

Letitia glanced at Frances, frowning. "At this early hour?"

"It must be something of importance."

Letitia rose, smoothing her gown. "I shall see what it is about."

As she walked gracefully to the drawing room, her happy thoughts about Philip did little to quell the unease that began to coil in her stomach. Upon entering, she was struck by the sight of the assembled company: Aunt Catherine, regal as ever in her emerald morning gown; Maria, her lovely features marred by a frown; Mrs. Trowbridge and Emily, seated stiffly on a settee. Near the fireplace stood Philip, his tall frame rigid. But it was the sight of Andrew Hargrove and his two younger ones that truly startled her.

Andrew? In London? What were they doing here?

She froze, and for some reason she could not understand, her heart began thrumming. Possibly it was because of the solemn atmosphere in the room. She curtsied before turning to the unexpected visitors.

"Andrew, what are you doing here?" she demanded quietly.

Andrew, a lean man with sandy hair and a thin-lipped mouth, rose from his chair with an icy demeanor that astounded her. Before he could speak, Maria interjected with sweetness. "So, you do know him, Letitia?"

"Yes," Letitia replied shortly. "He is Andrew Hargrove, from Brookstone. We were... friends."

Was it her imagination or did Philip stiffen?

Andrew's shrill smile twisted into something bitter. "Friends? Is that all I am to you now, Lettie, my love?"

She gasped. "Your love? Why are you here, Andrew?"

"I am here," he began, his voice ringing with righteous indignation, "to reveal the truth about you."

Her confusion deepened. "The truth? What truth?"

Andrew turned to the gathered company. "This woman," he said, pointing a finger at her, "is no heiress. She is a fraud!"

The room erupted into murmurs, but Letitia barely heard them. Her legs felt as though they might give way beneath her. "What are you talking about?"

Andrew pointed at the locket at her neck—the very locket that had been the key to her claim. "That is mine. It belonged to my late mother. I gave it to Letitia, in what I thought was an act of love. She took it and came to London, spinning a tale to claim the Barrington inheritance."

"That is a lie!" Letitia cried. "The locket was my mother's. Why are you doing this, Andrew?"

Andrew's brown eyes darkened with anger. "Because you have taken what does not belong to you! I trusted you, Letitia, and you have repaid me with deceit."

Letitia's gaze darted to Philip, and her heart sank at the stoniness on his face. "Philip," she called desperately, "you cannot believe this."

He did not reply as his gaze was locked on Andrew.

Andrew carried on. "I told Letitia the story of my mother and her first husband, The Marquess of Harrowfield, never imagining she would use it to fabricate a claim. When I read of the Barringtons' search for the heiress, I considered coming forward to set the record straight. But Letitia convinced me otherwise, concocting a scheme to present herself as the lost granddaughter. I refused to be part of such dishonesty and told her to desist from such treachery. She agreed. Then, a few days later, she told me she and her mother would be visiting a sick aunt for a while. And yet, here she is."

Letitia shook her head vehemently. "You are lying! You are doing this because I rejected your proposal. Is this your revenge, Andrew?"

"I am doing this," he answered coldly, "because it is the right thing to do. Oliver, Mary," he added, turning to his brother and sister, "you know this to be true. You were there."

All eyes turned to his siblings, who stood at the edge of the room with their heads bowed. "Yes." Oliver nodded. "The locket belonged to Mama."

Letitia drew in a strident breath, feeling as if she was still lying on her bed and having this awful nightmare.

"Ollie!" she cried, but he refused to look at her.

"Mary, you knew she planned to come here," Andrew went on, staring at his sister. "You knew she intended to deceive this family. You told me you overheard our conversation."

"Yes," Mary concurred in a small voice. "She wanted the money for herself, even when you begged her not to have such thoughts. She—"

"That is enough!" Letitia snapped, sickened by their lies. "You are all lying. Who put you up to this, Andrew? Do I deserve this cruelty from you? You have no proof, only your lies. None!"

Andrew's gaze bore into hers. "The proof is in the locket and in your lies. And my brother and sister here just attested to it. As a matter of fact, the entire Brookstone family can attest to the fact that Mrs. Robinson is your mother, not your aunt as you have falsely claimed. Where is Frances, your sister? Bring her to testify, too. She was the one who told me what you were up to."

Letitia paled. "Frances told you I—"

He smirked. "Yes. How do you think I found out what you and your mother did? She told me your plan and everything. She was ashamed to come from a house of swindlers."

Letitia's shoulders slumped as she wondered why Frances would lie against her? Was it out of jealousy? Seeing the condemning pairs of eyes before her, she turned to the only person who would believe her and the only person whose opinion of her mattered.

"Philip, please. You have known me for some weeks now. Surely, you know I would never do such a thing."

Philip's face was an unreadable mask, and he said nothing.

"Philip," she whispered, covering the distance between them. "You promised me... promised to stand by me. You told me your family was trying to find ways to sabotage me, that you would no longer side with them. Was that a lie?"

His silence was deafening, making her frantic.

"Please, believe me. I did not lie. I do not know why Andrew is doing this or who is making him do this, but you must know that I am indeed a Barrington. Show me the love you have been professing to me."

Aunt Catherine rose, her posture as imperious as ever. "This has gone on long enough, Letitia. Have you no shame? Philip is no longer blinded by your beauty and charm. He has seen you for the charlatan that you are. You will leave this house at once!"

Letitia's heart shattered at her aunt's word. "Philip," she pleaded, "look at me. Look at me and tell me you do not believe me."

He finally shifted his gaze to meet hers, but the coldness in his eyes froze her to the core. "I am sorry, Letitia. I do not know what to believe. The evidence is too incriminating."

Something died inside her. "I see. You do not know what to believe or you do not want to believe me because this arrangement suits you just fine?"

He frowned.

"With me out of the way, the inheritance is now yours, is it not? That was all you ever wanted, was it not?"

His face darkened, but he said nothing.

Her hands balled into fists at her sides. "Very well. I shall leave. I regret ever knowing all of you."

With that, she turned and fled the room, her heart breaking into a thousand pieces.

Chapter 18: Philip

The rain pattered faintly against the windows of Philip's study. For three days, he had been grappling with the heaviness of betrayal, or was it regret? The air within the room hung heavy with the scent of leather-bound books and the faint traces of the brandy he had yet to touch on his desk.

He sat slouched in his chair, fingers steepled under his chin, his troubled blue eyes fixed on the smoldering embers in the fireplace. The accusations against Letitia had been implicating, but a gnawing unease told him something was terribly amiss. He had even questioned the private investigator who found Andrew, but he had repeated the same thing: Letitia was a consummate schemer.

Philip had the mind to go to Brookstone to make his own inquiries, but what would that achieve? He would only be hurting himself more deeply if the evidence proved Letitia was indeed a liar. But his heart told him she was innocent.

Did I make a colossal blunder by not taking sides with her?

The door opening drew him from his thoughts. His brothers strode in with matching grave expressions. Philip sighed inwardly, having an idea why they were there. He had not been himself since the incident at the Barringtons'. He barely ate or slept, and he could not concentrate on his business. He had not even stepped a foot outside the townhouse since that day.

"Philip," James broke the silence in his baritone voice. "This moping does not suit you. You are the Duke of Wynthorpe, not some lovesick schoolboy."

Philip scowled. "Do not presume to lecture me. If you have come to show jubilation over the inheritance, save yourself the trouble. I care not a whit for it."

James exchanged a glance with Charles before sighing. "We are not here about the inheritance, you stubborn oaf. We are concerned about you. You have locked yourself in this study for days, shunning everyone. Letitia is gone; you should be relieved."

"Relieved?" Philip's voice rose, anger crossing his features. "She was not just anyone, James. She—" He stopped himself, looking away as if ashamed of the crack in his composure. "She meant everything to me."

"Then why did you let her go?" Charles asked softly, stepping closer. "If you believe she is a charlatan, that is one thing. But if you do not, then why are you not fighting for her?"

Philip closed his eyes and pinched the bridge of his nose. He thought of the tears in Letitia's eyes, the tremor in her voice as she begged him to believe her. Yet, the accusations against her had been so unfavorable. The blasted Andrew's words had rung like the toll of a death knell. The private investigator had confirmed the tale, adding to an already tangled mess.

"Because," he said at last, opening his eyes, "the evidence speaks for itself."

James crossed his arms, unimpressed. "And your heart, Philip? Does that not speak louder?"

The silence that followed was telling. He raked his fingers through his hair.

"Methinks if you love her so much, you should go and confront her and find out the truth instead of engaging in self-pity," Charles advised solemnly.

His heart longed to see Letitia, but he feared to be taken in by her again if she was not who she said she was.

"I shall think about it," he acquiesced to satisfy his brothers and wipe the frowns from their faces.

Later that afternoon, Emily arrived, her bright countenance a blunt disparity to Philip's brooding. She wore a peach gown embellished with ribbons, and her bonnet was perched at a jaunty angle. She clasped her gloved hands together as she surveyed him critically.

"Philip, you look positively ghastly. Have you even eaten today?"

He waved her off, muttering, "I am quite well."

"Hardly," she said tartly. "And you shall not wallow here another moment. There is a birthday gathering at the Wilkersons' tomorrow, and you will accompany me."

"I have no interest in such frivolities."

"Frivolities?" Emily arched a carved eyebrow. "Do not pretend you have grown too grim for society. You need a distraction, Philip, and I will brook no argument."

With a grudging sigh, he agreed just to get her out of his hair.

The next day, Philip found himself amidst the vibrant throng at the Wilkerson estate. The magnificent ballroom glittered with chandeliers, their golden light illuminating a sea of finely dressed guests. He wore a dark brown coat with silver buttons and a crisp white cravat, gold vest and biscuit brown trousers, but the fine clothes did little to mask his dour visage.

He exchanged polite nods with acquaintances, though he avoided conversations that might drift towards Letitia. Her absence hit him like a piercing ache that refused to be soothed as he recalled the soirees they had attended together. He longed to leave, but then he would only go home to continue brooding.

By evening, he slipped away to the gardens, seeking solitude. The cool air was a relief after the stifling atmosphere of the ballroom. The hedges were neatly trimmed, and the scent of jasmine filled the air. As he strolled along the path, voices reached his ears.

"You had best pay me, or I shall tell everyone the truth about Lady Letitia," a man growled.

Philip froze, recognizing the voice of his private investigator.

"I have been trying to seek your audience for days, but you refused to grant my request," the man carried on angrily. "And now I must come here, of all places, to demand what is owed?"

There was a muffled reply, too quiet for Philip to discern. The shadows ahead shifted, and he caught sight of the private investigator gesturing furiously.

Curiosity and suspicion propelled Philip forward. He moved silently, his boots crunching softly on the ground. As he neared, the second figure darted into the arbor, their identity concealed by the shadows. The private investigator turned to leave, but Philip stepped into his path, blocking his escape.

"Not so fast, Hamilton," Philip said coldly. "You will explain yourself."

The man stiffened, his eyes wide with alarm. "Your Grace, I—"

"Spare me the excuses," Philip snapped. "I heard enough to know you are up to something nefarious. Who hired you, and what lies have you been peddling against Lady Letitia?"

"Your Grace, nothing—"

"Very well, then. If you do not tell me, perhaps you will speak to the authorities. Let us go!" His grip on the man's arm tightened.

Hamilton dithered, his gaze darting towards the arbor before returning to Philip. "All right, Your Grace. I was hired," he admitted grudgingly. "To investigate Lady Letitia... and to provide... a certain narrative."

"And this narrative," Philip deduced icily, "included fabricating evidence against her?"

The man swallowed hard. "The lad, Andrew, was all too eager to talk ill of her. He felt slighted, you see. He claimed she turned down his proposal, and he wanted to get even with her. So, it was easy to feed him what he would say."

Good Lord! How could I have allowed myself to be deceived again concerning Letitia? Oh, my love, I have failed you yet again.

"And who hired you?" Philip demanded. "Do not think to protect them."

The private investigator's face contorted with fear. "I do not know their name, Your Grace. Only that they wished to claim the inheritance for themselves."

"But you were speaking to someone just now."

"Yes, but only in the shadows. The person is a messenger, too. I could not recognize the voice."

Philip's mind started pointing with possibilities. The details, the timing—it all pointed to someone with intimate knowledge of the Barrington affairs and someone who wanted Letitia gone at all costs. And then, a chilling realization struck him.

Aunt Catherine!

He released the investigator with a sharp shove. "Be gone. If I ever see you again, I will ensure you face the full wrath of the law."

The man fled, and Philip smirked. He would have Bow Street runners pick up Hamilton in the morning and made to confess the name of his hirer. But for now, he had a cousin to confront. He turned back towards the house, his thoughts in a maelstrom.

What had he done? Would Letitia ever forgive him? Anguish filled him as he remembered the tears in her eyes as she begged for him to believe her. Inwardly, deep inside his soul, he had known she was innocent, but why he had not acted in her favor astounded him. When she needed him the most, he had turned his back on her.

Some love I claim to profess. When I needed to show it, I failed miserably. I shall make everything right posthaste.

As he re-entered the ballroom, his gaze swept the crowd until it landed on Aunt Catherine. She strode towards the refreshment table, having just entered the ballroom through another door.

What other proof did he need?

He approached her with purposeful strides. By the time he reached her, she had a glass of champagne in hand, her face calm, but to Philip, it was a mask of deceit.

"Aunt Catherine," he said in a clipped tone. "A word."

She turned, feigning surprise. "Philip, what is the matter?"

"You know very well what the matter is," he riposted angrily. "I overheard everything in the garden. Your hired lackey confessed to fabricating evidence against Letitia. I know you were the one who orchestrated it."

Her face paled, but she quickly composed herself. "I have no idea what you are talking about."

"Do not lie to me," he hissed. "Your scheme has unraveled, and you will leave the Barrington household immediately."

Her lips tightened, and for a moment, he thought she might deny it further. Instead, she sniffed disdainfully. "You are a fool, Philip. To keep choosing a stranger over your family. I did nothing wrong. But if you want me gone, so be it! I will not beg you. But just you know, that girl will bring you nothing but ruin."

"Enough! You will go and not return until you learn to accept your late father's dictates!"

Without waiting for her reply, he turned on his heel and left the ballroom. His fury was more against himself than her. He should have known better, given all she had done to discredit Letitia.

As he swung into his carriage, he knew what had to be done. He would go to Brookstone and make amends with Letitia… if she would have him.

Chapter 19: Letitia

"It is all right, Fran. Please stop crying. You cried all the way back to Brookstone and have been doing so ever since. You will make yourself sick."

Letitia sat on the edge of the modest bed in the room she shared with Frances at Brookstone. Frances, red-eyed and crumpled like a wilted flower, clutched a handkerchief and sobbed into her hands.

"How can I stop feeling so wretched, Lettie? I thought Andrew cared for me," Frances hiccupped, explaining herself for the umpteenth time. "He seemed so kind. I never knew it was just a ploy to get information about you. I truly believed he might offer for me. I did not know he was in love with you, and you had rejected his proposal."

Letitia smoothed her cousin's hair, her own emotions tightly coiled within. Her charcoal brown gown, slightly worn at the hem, swished as she shifted to face Frances. She had abandoned all the lovely dresses back in London.

"You could not have known his intentions," Letitia said softly. "Andrew's duplicity has hurt us both, but do not let it poison your heart."

Frances lifted her tear-streaked face. "But it is my fault! I told him everything. When I informed him that we were leaving for London, he demanded to know why, but I did not tell him. Then he said that if I loved him, I would trust him with the secret. I felt so guilty that I told him, but I never knew he would use it to revenge against you. I trusted him, and now... now he has ruined things for you."

"Enough," Letitia said firmly. She wished Frances had confided in her about her feelings for Andrew, but she could not tell her that, for the younger girl already felt remorseful enough. "What is done cannot be undone. I forgive you, Fran. Truly. Andrew alone is to blame for his lies."

Frances flung her arms around Letitia, who returned the embrace with a trembling sigh. Andrew's betrayal was nothing compared to the man she loved. The man who had claimed to love her, who had filled her days with joy and laughter and her nights with dreams, had cast her aside without a second thought.

I feel so foolish. I should have listened to Emily and Maria when they warned me about his true intentions. But I allowed love to becloud my senses.

Letitia disentangled herself gently from Frances's arms, needing the solace of solitude. She fetched her shawl, a faded but comforting woolen wrap, and slipped out of the cottage.

The late afternoon sun bathed Brookstone in golden hues as she walked to the pond at the edge of the village. This small haven, surrounded by weeping willows and the gentle hum of nature, had always been her refuge.

Seated on the bank, she hugged her knees and gazed into the water. Her reflection stared back at her, eyes puffy from tears she had not wanted Frances to see. Memories of Philip flooded her mind—his teasing smile, the warmth in his stunning blue eyes, the way he had made her feel as though she were the center of his world.

But that world had crumbled. He had made her believe he truly loved her when he was only after her wealth. Well, she was not wealthy anymore; she had been thrown out of her grandfather's house like a common criminal.

I hope your conscience pricks you anytime you spend my grandfather's money, Philip.

A sound behind her snapped her from her reverie. She stiffened, wondering if Frances had followed her there. She knew her cousin was sorry for her part, but she did not want to listen to her apologies any longer. Before she could open her mouth to tell her to leave, a familiar voice called out.

"Letitia."

She inhaled sharply and shook her head. No, she must be imagining it. She clutched her shawl tighter, refusing to look back.

How pathetic for me to still be imagining his voice.

"Letitia, please," the voice came again, closer now.

She rose abruptly, spinning around. And there he was. Philip. Tall and broad-shouldered, dressed in a navy coat and buff-colored breeches, his hair slightly disheveled as though he had run his fingers repeatedly through it.

Her heart betrayed her with a leap of joy before she crushed the feeling under layers of wounded pride.

Is it my eyes, or has he lost some weight?

"What are you doing here?" she demanded curtly, though her fingers shook as she tightened the shawl around her shoulders.

Exhaling loudly, he closed the gap between them. He stared at her with an intensity that made her want to look away and yet rooted her in place.

"I came to find you," he said simply. "I need to speak with you."

She forced a laugh, though it sounded hollow to her own ears. "You have had your say, Philip. Your silence said it all. There is nothing more to discuss."

"There is everything to discuss," he replied in a fervent tone. "I was a fool to let you go, Letitia. A blind, stubborn fool."

"Indeed," she said coolly, though her throat constricted. "And yet here you are, after all is said and done. Why? Have you tired of *my* inheritance already?"

He flinched but took another step forward. "Do not speak as though you do not know me."

"Do I?" she retorted heatedly. "The man I thought I knew would not have turned his back on me so easily, would not have—" Her voice cracked, and she pressed a hand to her mouth.

"I was wrong," he confessed. "Wrong to doubt you, wrong to listen to lies when my heart told me otherwise. I am so sorry. Please forgive me."

Her eyes narrowed. "And what has brought about this miraculous revelation?"

He looked down, a shadow passing over his face. "I wish I could say I listened to my heart when it told me you were innocent of the accusations levelled against you, but I am afraid that was not the case." He sighed before carrying on. "I overheard a conversation between my private investigator and someone. When I confronted him, he confessed he was paid to fabricate evidence against you and to coax Andrew into lying."

She stared at him, nonplussed. "And who orchestrated this farce?"

"I suspect Aunt Catherine," he answered with anger in his eyes. "Though she denied it, I heard enough to know she played a part."

Relief wafted through her that the truth was out at last. But then it was quickly replaced by ire. She crossed her arms and regarded him with infuriation. "And now, armed with this truth, you expect me to forgive you? To return to London and play the fool once more?"

"No," he said quietly.

She blinked. "No?"

He drew abreast, the honesty she read his eyes making her heart ache. "I do not care about London, the inheritance, or the title. I care about you, Letitia. Only you."

She shook her head. "You said that once before. How am I to believe you now?"

"Because I will prove it," he said earnestly. "If you will not believe words, then believe actions. I am prepared to renounce the title, the wealth—everything. All of it means nothing without you."

Her breath left her in a rush, and she stared at him, searching his face for any hint of deceit. "You would give up everything? For me?"

"Yes," he said without hesitation. "Marry me, Letitia, and see that I do not care about your money. As a matter of fact, I relinquish the title and everything to do with the Barrington name... well, except yours, of course. That way, I am no longer entitled to a single dime; for you to see that I care about only *you*." He lifted his hand to run it through his ruffled hair. "It was very wrong of me not to have stood by you even after promising I would always do that. I know I have no excuse for hurting you, but at the time, the evidence against you seemed so damning, I was at a crossroad about what to believe. But I swear to you this day, now that I know what my family is capable of and how far they will go to discredit you, you will always have my trust... and my love. Forever."

Emotion surged within her—hope, fear, disbelief. She looked away, her gaze falling on the rippling surface of the pond. She desperately wanted to accept his words, but she was afraid of getting hurt again. "You wounded me deeply, Philip. I trusted you, and you cast me aside as though I were nothing."

"I know," he said with remorse. "I know, and I will spend the rest of my life making it up to you, if you will allow me."

Tears stung her eyes, but she blinked them away. "It is not so simple. Trust cannot be mended with mere words."

"Then let me prove myself," he implored, stepping closer still. "Say you will give me a chance."

She chewed on her bottom lip as her heart warred with her head. Could she dare to believe him?

"I do not know if I can."

He reached for her hand. "Then I will wait. As long as it takes. I will wait."

"Very well," she said at last. "But do not think I will make it easy for you."

A faint smile curved his lips. "I would expect nothing less."

She stared at him, wondering if she was making another grave mistake by listening to him. He could be lying again for all she knew. But why was he here and willing to forsake it all for her? Well, time would tell if his intentions were genuine.

Chapter 20: Philip

Philip adjusted the fishing rod in his hand, a wide grin spreading across his face as the line tugged and dipped. He stared at the rippling surface of the pond, reflecting shades of gold and green from the sunlight. Letitia stood a few feet away, the gentle breeze teasing a loose curl from beneath her bonnet. She watched him with amusement, and her lips remained in that soft, unreadable smile he had come to cherish.

"Steady, Philip," she told him with a playful tilt of her head. "You would not wish to frighten the poor creatures off with your enthusiasm."

Philip chuckled as he focused on the task at hand. "Let us hope my skill matches my enthusiasm, then. I should hate for you to think me incapable of mastering a simple pastime like fishing."

Letitia's laugh was melodic, and it warmed him more than the sun ever could. "Fishing is hardly a skill one perfects in a week. Though, I must admit, you have taken to country life rather well for someone who once balked at the thought of milking a cow."

He cast her a sidelong glance, his grin widening. "You must admit, Letitia, my cow-milking was nothing short of exceptional. I daresay I surprised even myself."

Her lips twitched as she fought to keep a straight face. "Yes, if you consider narrowly avoiding being kicked a mark of mastery."

He burst into laughter, blissfully recounting the past week that he had been there. He had been having the most wonderful time of his life, enjoying the simple lifestyle the countryside presented. He had learned how to milk a cow, collected eggs from angry hens, killed a chicken, and gone riding every morning with Letitia. Her family had welcomed him warmly, even though he believed her Aunt Helen was still wary of him. He had told them to stop calling him by his title because he was now a commoner like them. And he loved it.

Before he could retort, the line jerked harder, and with a triumphant whoop, he reeled in his prize—a modest-sized fish that flopped indignantly on the grass.

"Behold!" he declared, holding it aloft for Letitia's inspection. "A feast fit for a king... or, in this case, a former duke turned humble fisherman."

Letitia clapped her hands lightly, her smile widening. "Well done, Philip. At this rate, the village may indeed adopt you as one of their own."

Her words warmed his heart as he stared at her. He realized he was now more in love with her than ever. But he was worried that she might not feel the same way about him because she had rejected his proposal of marriage and never responded when he told her he loved her. He had thought she reciprocated his feelings when they were in London, but now, he was not so sure. Maybe not believing her had killed her love for him. He resolved to work harder to show her how much he loved her and make her love him again.

LETITIA, THE RIGHTFUL HEIR 141

As her laughter faded, her expression turned contemplative. His mirth dimmed as he noted the sudden change in her demeanor. He set the fish aside and drew closer, his boots crunching softly against the grassy bank.

"You have gone quiet suddenly," he said gently. "What troubles you, Letitia?"

She lifted her eyes to meet his. "Philip, as much as I have enjoyed these days with you, we cannot continue like this indefinitely. You must return to London."

His forehead furrowed. "Return to London? Without you? Absolutely not."

"You must," she insisted. "We cannot let whoever sought to ruin me win. You have responsibilities, and I—"

"I have responsibilities to you," he interrupted. "Letitia, I left London not to escape my title or duties but to prove to you that you mean more to me than any of it. I am not going anywhere without you."

She shook her head, exasperation mingling with the faintest hint of a smile. "You cannot abandon your life for mine, Philip. It is neither practical nor fair."

"Practicality be cursed," he shot back. "If you will not return with me, then I shall remain here. I will learn to farm or take up carpentry—though, I must warn you, I have no natural talent for woodwork."

The absurdity of his declaration broke through her seriousness, and she laughed—a light, genuine sound that made his chest tighten. "You, a farmer? A carpenter? I cannot imagine it."

"Can you not?" He grinned, seizing on her moment of levity. "Perhaps I shall build you the finest cottage in the village, complete with a pond stocked with fish that leap willingly into our nets."

"Philip!" she exclaimed, laughing harder now.

Encouraged, he pressed on. "And I shall grow the most bountiful garden, filled with roses to rival the ones in London. You will see. I am nothing if not determined."

Her laughter faded, though her smile stayed on her lips. She regarded him for a moment. "You are irredeemable, Philip."

"That is not a no," he pointed out, then he became serious. "Letitia, please believe me when I say that I love you and will not go back without you. If you really want me gone, then come back with me. Let us face the enemy together."

She sighed and kept silent for a long moment. He kept a blank face, but his heart hammered against his chest. His businesses were suffering as well as some affairs relating to his duties as the former duke, but he did not want to be without Letitia. Yes, he was not accustomed to this lifestyle, but he could get used to it. After all, he had never really fancied the intricacies of the upper-class.

"Very well," she finally said, and he exhaled with pent-up relief. "But on one condition."

"Name it," he said immediately.

"We visit Andrew before returning," she said. "If there is any chance of learning who orchestrated this plot against us, we must take it."

He nodded with a smile. "Agreed. Together, we will uncover the truth."

***

Two days later, Philip and Letitia stood outside a modest house in the village. Andrew's older brother, Matthew, greeted them at the door, his expression wary but polite.

"I am afraid you have come in vain," he said, moving aside to allow them entry. "Andrew has gone."

Philip frowned. "Gone? Do you mean he has left the village entirely?"

He nodded, his mouth set in a grim line. "He departed not long after Miss Letitia returned and word spread of his involvement in the false accusations. I fear he was ashamed, or perhaps fearful of the repercussions."

Letitia frowned. "Do you know where he went?"

"I do not," he acknowledged, his gaze shifting to the floor. "He spoke little before leaving. He was deeply hurt by... certain events."

Letitia's face crumbled with sadness. "You mean my rejection of his proposal?"

The older man faltered, then nodded. "It wounded his pride, yes. But I believe there was more to it. He seemed troubled, as though burdened by a weight he could not share."

Philip exchanged a glance with Letitia. He understood how Andrew felt over losing Letitia, but he would never have hurt her the way he did. "Do you know if he confided in anyone? Mentioned anyone who might have influenced him?"

Matthew shook his head. "No, though I suspect someone preyed on his vulnerabilities. He was not one to act maliciously."

Letitia nodded. "That is true. Thank you."

As they departed, Philip placed a hand on her arm. "We will find him, Letitia. And whoever is behind this will face justice."

She nodded, though her gaze remained distant. "I only hope Andrew finds peace. I never intended to cause him pain."

Philip tightened his grip slightly, drawing her attention back to him. "You are not to blame for his choices, Letitia. Remember that."

Her lips curved into a faint smile. "Thank you, Philip."

Later that evening, as they prepared to return to London, Philip caught Letitia gazing out the window of the small parlor.

"Penny for your thoughts?" he asked, settling beside her on the bench.

She glanced at him. "I was thinking of what lies ahead. There is so much uncertainty."

He reached for her hand, and his fingers curled around hers. "Whatever lies ahead, we will face it together. I swear to you, I will never let you face anything alone again."

Her eyes glistened, and she blinked away the moisture before it could fall. "You are quite determined, are you not?"

He smiled, his thumb brushing lightly over her knuckles. "For you, my love, I am unstoppable."

She returned his smile. "Then let us see what the future holds."

The following day, as his ducal carriage began its journey, Philip felt a renewed sense of purpose. He had lost her trust once but vowed never to do so again. With Letitia by his side, he knew they could face any challenge from his family or whoever, and, perhaps, find the happiness they both deserved.

Chapter 21: Letitia

Letitia leaned back against the plush cushions of Philip's ducal carriage, her gloved fingers absently tracing the fine embroidery on the armrest. Opposite her, Philip reclined in an air of effortless elegance, his hair slightly wind-swept from their journey. Frances, acting as her ever-dutiful chaperone, sat beside Letitia, her knitting needles clicking softly as the carriage wheels rattled over the uneven road.

"Your carriage is most impressive, Your... er... Philip," Frances remarked, blushing. "One cannot deny it was crafted for a man of importance."

Philip smiled faintly. "It served its purpose in London, I suppose, though now it feels a touch excessive. One cannot easily navigate the country lanes in such a cumbersome contraption."

Letitia arched an eyebrow with a glint in her eyes. "Yet you insisted we travel in it. Were you hoping to intimidate the good villagers of... what is the name of the town we are heading to again?" she asked teasingly, even though she knew the name. Along the way, they had decided to visit the village where her mother and aunt had lived before the latter took her away. They hoped they would find more proof to show that she was indeed the heiress to silence their family once and for all.

"Westridge," Philip supplied, the corners of his mouth twitching upwards. "And I thought it might offer some comfort, though I see now that it may only highlight my folly."

"Indeed," she replied lightly. "You are fortunate the villagers of Brookstone were forgiving of your... initial inadequacies."

He placed a hand over his heart in mock affront. "I shall have you know that milking a cow is a far more complex undertaking than one might assume. And I seem to recall you praised my persistence."

She laughed tenderly. "You were persistent, I grant you that. Even Aunt Helen, who was quite prepared to dislike you, has conceded that your intentions are genuine."

He grinned. "I would hope so, Letitia. I have done all in my power to prove it to you."

Her heart quickened, but she turned her attention to the window, where rolling fields and the occasional cluster of cottages blurred past. She could no longer deny that she was still very much in love with Philip and had grown to greatly admire him after the week he spent in Brookstone as a commoner. The villagers, who had been in awe to have a duke amongst them, had quickly gotten used to his presence. A smile crossed her face when she remembered how the young girls in the village fawned over him anytime they went for walks. Indeed, Aunt Helen had initially been wary of him but had come to like him a lot and had told her that she sensed his feelings for her were genuine.

"Tell me about the Wynthorpe estate," she said, seeking to shift the conversation. "You mentioned a little about its history earlier. What secrets does it hold?"

He nodded, still smiling. "Wynthorpe has stood for over three centuries, though the Barrington family's claim to it began with my great-great-grandfather. He purchased the estate from a marquess who had gambled away his fortune."

"How resourceful of him," she said, intrigued.

"Resourceful, indeed," he agreed, a hint of pride in his tone. "He was a shrewd man and saw potential where others did not. The estate flourished under his care, and subsequent generations expanded its reach."

"And now it is under your care," she mentioned with a smile. Then she frowned. "How did you come to inherit the dukedom, by the way?"

He shrugged. "It is a rather convoluted tale, but I shall endeavor to simplify it. Your grandfather and my grandmother were siblings. When your grandfather passed, the title was supposed to pass to your father, but he was deceased. With no other male heirs, it was then reverted to the cousin who was the eldest male relative, and therefore next in line. It would have been my father but since he is also deceased, it fell to me," he explained quietly.

She studied him. "It must be a great responsibility to bear."

"It is," he admitted resignedly. "But it is a responsibility I have come to accept. And now, my priority is ensuring that justice is done for you, Letitia."

She nodded and looked out of the window. She was tempted to seek for more, to ask about the Henshaws, but she sensed he was keeping something from her. And she did not want to appear too inquisitive.

By the time they reached Westridge, the sun had dropped lower over the quaint village. Narrow cobbled streets wound between stone cottages festooned with flowers and herbs. As they disembarked from the carriage, curious eyes peered from behind lace curtains, and children paused in their play to gawk at the grand vehicle.

"Well," Letitia murmured, smoothing her skirts, "it appears we have made an impression."

Philip offered his arm, his smile faintly amused. "Let us hope it is a favorable one."

They inquired at the local inn and were directed to a small cottage on the outskirts of the village. The dwelling was modest but well-kept, with a neatly tended garden bursting with late spring blooms. Letitia swallowed thickly with emotion as she stared at the house where she had been birthed. As if sensing her discomfiture, Philip reached out to take her hand and squeezed it.

An elderly woman opened the door, her lined face breaking into a warm smile as she took them in. Her gaze seemed rooted on Letitia for minutes on end, which made her uncomfortable.

"Good day," Philip greeted respectfully. "We were hoping to speak with you about a matter of some importance."

The woman ushered them inside, gesturing to a cozy parlor furnished with mismatched but comfortable chairs. "You will forgive me, I hope, if I ask your names before we proceed. It is not every day I receive such distinguished visitors."

"I am Philip Henshaw," he said, inclining his head. "And this is Lady Letitia Barrington."

The woman's eyes widened. "Barrington, you say? My, my. You must be Lady Clara's daughter. I should have guessed upon first seeing you. You look just like her, save for your eyes, which resemble your father's."

Letitia gasped. "You knew my mother? And my father?"

"Oh, indeed," the woman replied with a nostalgic smile. "I was in service to her, hired by your father, The Marquess of Harrowfield. A kinder soul you could not hope to meet."

Tears pricked Letitia's eyes, but she forced herself to focus. "Can you tell us about her? And about the Lord Harrowfield?"

The older woman nodded. "I'm Lucy. I was hired as a companion and maid to her ladyship, but after her passing, I remained to care for the house." A wistful smile crossed her face. "Lord Harrowfield held his wife in great esteem, even though they married in secret. They were very much in love, and it was such a shame that circumstances kept them apart."

Letitia batted her eyelids to keep back tears as the older woman went on and on about her parents and their love for each other despite how brief their union was. Letitia smiled as it was apparent how deeply her parents had cared for each other. It was indeed a disservice to two people so much in love to be kept apart because of status.

"Was she ever acknowledged as his wife?" Philip asked gently.

She shook her head. "Not formally because of his father, but he treated her as such in every respect. When she passed, it broke him." She frowned. "What brings you here?"

Philip briefly explained about her grandfather's will. The woman nodded knowingly.

Letitia's throat bobbed with emotion. "Would you be willing to come to London and testify to her relationship with my father and that I am their daughter?"

She sighed, her frail hands twisting in her lap. "I am afraid my traveling days are long behind me, my lady. But I can write you a letter, attesting to all that I know."

Philip nodded. "That would be most helpful. Thank you."

***

As the carriage rattled back towards London, Letitia sat in contemplative silence, thinking about her parents and all that the old woman told them.

"She must have been remarkable," she murmured, her gaze static on the passing landscape. "I mean, for my father to have fallen in love with her, defied his stern father, and married her."

"By all accounts, she was," Philip replied affectionately. "And so was your father. He was a man of honor, forced to make impossible choices but never wavering in his love for your mother."

Tears brimmed in her eyes. Silently, Frances reached for her hand and squeezed it before pulling her into her embrace and whispering comforting words to her. When Letitia was in control of her emotions again, she sat up and dabbed at her eyes with the handkerchief Philip offered her.

"I wish I had known them. To have been loved by them," she whispered.

Philip reached for her other hand and caressed it. "You are loved, Letitia. By your aunt and her family... and by me."

A deep flush enveloped her. "Philip, I—"

"Do not feel compelled to say anything," he said gently. "I only wish for you to know the depth of my feelings."

She nodded and smiled through her tears. It might be difficult, given the obstacles before them, but she was determined that hers and Philip's love story would not end like that of her parents.

Chapter 22: Philip

Philip stood at the edge of the garden, his gloved hands resting on the wrought-iron railing, watching Letitia from a distance. She was seated on a stone bench beneath a grand oak, a book in her hands, though her attention appeared elsewhere. Her hair shimmered in the sunlight, and a delicate bonnet was perched atop her head with ribbons trailing down her back.

He had arrived early, drawn by an unrelenting need to see her again. It seemed ludicrous, given that they had spent the past fortnight together, but his heart had grown restless the moment they parted. She laughed at something Frances said before the younger woman excused herself, leaving Letitia alone with her book.

Philip's thoughts were in discordance. Had he done enough? Could he dare to ask her again? The first time had been disastrous because she had no longer trusted him. Now, with the truth revealed and his heart firmly in her grasp, he feared rejection anew. He itched to have it done with so no one would ever try to hurt her again, definitely not when she bore his name and was now a duchess.

Gathering his courage, he strode towards her. Letitia turned as he advanced, her face brightening with a smile that sent a jolt of hope through him.

At least she is delighted to see me.

"Philip," she greeted warmly, setting her book aside. "You are here early."

"I could not keep away," he confessed with a nervous smile. He gestured to the seat beside her. "May I?"

"Of course," she replied, moving to make space.

He sat, her proximity both a comfort and a torment, and breathed in her flowery fragrance. She wore a yellow gown accentuating the graceful lines of her slightly curvy figure.

"Are you not fatigued from our travels?" he asked, striving for casual conversation.

She shook her head, a lively glint in her eyes. "Not at all. The journey was pleasant enough, thanks to your impeccable arrangements. And yourself?"

"I—" He paused, then laughed tenderly. "I find myself rather restless."

Her forehead crinkled slightly. "Restless? Is something amiss?"

He took a deep breath, and his gaze fell to the patterned stones beneath their feet. "I wanted to speak with you, Letitia. To tell you, again how sorry I am for my behavior when last I proposed. I cannot excuse my mistrust, but I hope you can forgive it."

She smiled, and she reached out to lay a hand on his arm. "Philip, it is water under the bridge. We have both made mistakes. What matters is what lies ahead."

Her words emboldened him. "What lies ahead," he echoed, "is what I wish to speak of. Letitia, I love you. I love you with a depth I scarcely knew myself capable of. These past weeks have cemented what

I already knew. You are the only woman I ever wish to stand beside me, as my partner, my equal, and my duchess."

Her face flushed a delicate pink as he rose and went on a bended knee.

"Letitia Anne Barrington, will you do me the honor of becoming my wife?"

Please say yes. He hoped she could not hear his heart drumming erratically, for he feared she would say no.

To his utter astonishment, she smiled, her eyes shining with unabashed elation. "Yes, Philip. I will marry you. I love you, too."

For a moment, he could scarcely breathe, the sheer joy of her words overwhelming. Then, unable to contain himself, he rose and swept her into his arms, spinning her in an exuberant circle. She laughed, a sound of pure delight, and he placed a kiss on her cheek before setting her down.

"You have made me the happiest man in England," he declared proudly.

"And you have made me the happiest woman," she replied with a radiant smile.

He kissed her hands. "I want to spend the entire day with you, but there is something I must do, now that you have agreed to become my wife."

She peered at him with curiosity. "What could be more important than celebrating our betrothal together?"

He smiled. "Announcing it to the world. I must send word to the dailies of our impending nuptials. Let no one be in doubt anymore that you are the legitimate granddaughter and you are to become my duchess. Besides, I do not want a long betrothal. We should be married in less than two weeks."

She gasped. "Philip!"

He feigned innocence. "Yes, my love."

"I do not know how the upper-class get married, but I dare say a week is not enough for the preparations."

"Two then. Is that okay?" he grumbled.

She giggled helplessly. "I shall have to consult with Aunt Helen before I give you a reply."

He groaned. "Very well then, but three weeks is all the patience I can muster before I make you my wife." He exhaled quietly. "Now, I must leave you for a few hours."

She shrugged, obviously not wanting to let him go. "If you must."

"I must." Then his eyes darkened. "I will also have to visit Aunt Catherine and Maria to inform them. Even though I do not owe them an explanation, given what they did to you, they are still our family."

She nodded. "Of course."

He kissed her cheek. "I shall be back before you know it."

A dazzling smile lit her face. "I shall count every minute until you return."

It took everything in Philip to pull away after kissing her cheek again. He did not wish to part from her, but he had to put certain things in motion. As he strode away from the garden, he could hardly believe that she had accepted his proposal and even reciprocated his feelings. Indeed, he was the luckiest man in all of England.

***

That afternoon, Philip strode into the grand townhouse in Mayfair, where Aunt Catherine and Maria were staying as guests of Lady Fitzwilliam. He struggled with the guilt plaguing him that he had cast his relatives from their home, putting them at the mercy of Aunt

Catherine's friend. But it was what they deserved for trying to do the same thing to their own relative. If only they would just accept Letitia and stop plotting against her.

The butler admitted him, and Philip did not wait for an announcement before striding into the parlor where his cousins were seated.

"Philip." Aunt Catherine looked at him with surprise. "To what do we owe this unannounced visit?"

He wasted no time on pleasantries. "I am here to put an end to whatever schemes you may still harbor regarding Letitia."

Maria paled, her embroidery hoop slipping from her hands. Aunt Catherine, however, narrowed her eyes. "I do not know what you mean."

"Do not play coy," he responded, steely. "You have conspired to discredit her and to deny her rightful place as the heiress. Letitia is to be my wife, and I will not tolerate any further attempts to undermine her."

Maria gasped. "Your wife?"

"Yes, she has accepted my proposal."

Maria glanced nervously at her mother, who pursed her lips. "Philip, you must understand—"

"I understand perfectly," he interrupted. "Your ambitions for Maria will not come at Letitia's expense. If you wish to remain part of this family, you will accept her as my duchess and cease this nonsense at once."

Silence fell as the tension became palpable. When neither woman responded, Philip sighed.

"I have told you that I will take excellent care of you. If you are worried about Maria, I promise to provide her with a large dowry that would make her the most sought-after spinster in all of England. If you choose to live with us in the townhouse or in Wynthorpe, you will always be welcome. But if you prefer a private residence, I will provide it and grant you a monthly allowance that will see to all your needs. However, I shall do all these and more for you and our other relatives only if you stop being so bitter and vindictive. I have told you repeatedly that 'tis no fault of Letitia that she found herself in the situation." After letting that sink in, he added, "So, consider my words carefully. There will be no second warnings."

When he received no response, he nodded, turned and strode from the room. His betrothed was the most important person in his life at the moment, and he would protect her come rain, come shine. He had failed her before; he would not do so again.

Later, Philip called upon Mrs. Trowbridge, who had always been like family to him. She welcomed the news with warm congratulations.

"I am delighted for you," she happily told him. "Letitia is a fine young lady, and you are fortunate to have won her heart."

"I am well aware of my good fortune," he replied, smiling. "Thank you for your support."

"If you require assistance with the wedding preparations," she went on, "do not hesitate to call upon me. I am more than happy to step in if certain parties prove less cooperative."

He smiled wryly, appreciating her tactful phrasing. "Your offer is most welcome, Mrs. Trowbridge. I shall keep it in mind."

He had hoped to speak to Emily, wanting her to hear the news from him rather than from the dailies, but she was not in residence. He hoped she would take the news well, given that she had held affections for him that he had been blind to. He did not wish for her to be hurt, but he could not help the situation. He would never love her the way she wanted.

He had a delightful lunch with Letitia before leaving again to hire another private investigator to look for Andrew. He then visited the solicitor to reinstate Letitia as the heiress.

The following day, Philip prepared for the musicale where he and Letitia would make their first public appearance as a betrothed couple. He had planned to share the truth about his wealth with her, but they kept being interrupted. He enjoyed being captivated by the joy on her face as the *ton* offered their congratulations.

"You seem rather pleased with yourself," Emily teased as she met him at the door after the performance. Thankfully, she had accepted the news without any ill-feeling and was genuinely happy for them.

"I am," he said, his gaze fixed on Letitia, who was chatting gaily to an old couple. "And I intend to remain so for quite some time."

For now, the rest could wait. Watching Letitia's happiness was more than enough.

Chapter 23: Letitia

This is the happiest day of my life, but I cannot help being nervous. Letitia's heart raced as she sat before the ornate gilt-edged mirror in her dressing room. Today was her wedding day, the day she would marry Philip and begin a new chapter of her life. Despite her certainty about her feelings, a nervous flutter persisted in her chest.

"Hold still, my dear, or the maid shall never finish your hair," Aunt Helen chided gently, fussing over her.

Letitia smiled faintly and obediently held still until the maid was done and exited the room. Her wedding gown was an exquisite creation of ivory silk. The bodice was embellished with delicate silver thread in floral motifs, each petal and leaf catching the light. The neckline, simple but elegant, was framed by short, puffed sleeves trimmed with Chantilly lace. The skirts billowed in soft waves, flowing to the floor and ending in a small train. A satin sash, cinched at her waist, added a final touch of refinement.

"Oh, Lettie!" Frances exclaimed with admiration. "You look like an angel descended from heaven itself!"

Aunt Helen stepped back, nodding as she inspected her niece. "Indeed, you do. Philip is a fortunate man."

Letitia laughed softly, though her nerves persisted. "I hope he does not regret it."

"Regret it?" Frances gasped. "Nonsense. He is utterly besotted with you, as are we all."

Letitia's smile grew, and her mind drifted to the past four weeks. The days had been a flurry of wedding preparations and wonderful moments with Philip. He had been attentive, charming, and unrelenting in his efforts to ensure her happiness. They had traveled to Paris with Frances, Aunt Helen, and Mrs. Trowbridge for her wedding trousseau and had the most wonderful time there.

The memory of all the time they spent together attending balls, luncheons, Venetian breakfasts, the theatre, and musicales still warmed her. Everyone had wanted them to attend their soirées and had complimented them on how much they were in love with each other. But sudden fear gripped her. Her parents had also loved each other immensely, but they had not had a happy ending. Could happiness this perfect last? She worried that something would go wrong that could tear them apart. Aunt Catherine and Maria had not done anything to sabotage their wedding preparations thus far, but their absence showed their displeasure.

She chewed on her bottom lip, for she did not like that the family was divided. However, a great many other relatives had shown their support, and the house was full of wedding gifts and visitors. Although Philip hid it, she knew he was not happy that his closest cousins would not be in attendance. On her part, she had written to Aunt Catherine and Maria since they refused to grant her audience when she went visiting, asking for their support, but she got no response. At least the solicitor had reinstated her as the heiress without question.

A knock at the door interrupted her thoughts, and a young maid poked her head in. "Begging your pardon, my lady." She turned to Aunt Helen. "Mrs. Robinson, your neighbors from the countryside have just arrived. They are asking for you."

Aunt Helen looked surprised but rose immediately. "I shall return shortly, my dear."

No sooner had Aunt Helen departed than another knock came. This time, it was another maid addressing Frances. "Miss Frances, Mrs. Trowbridge wishes to speak with you. She said it is urgent."

Frances frowned, glancing at Letitia. "Will you be all right on your own, Lettie?"

"I will be fine," Letitia assured her, managing a small smile.

When Frances left, the silence settled heavily in the room, broken only by the ticking of the clock on the mantel. Letitia's gaze shifted to her reflection, searching for reassurance in her own eyes. And then joy spread through her heart.

"I am marrying Philip today," she whispered with a bright smile. She could hardly wait to be his wife. She loved him so much she could not bear to think of life without him.

The door creaked open, and Letitia turned, expecting to see either Aunt Helen or Frances. Instead, it was Emily, her mien a blend of mockery and smugness as she sauntered into the room. Letitia had hardly seen her during the wedding preparations, and she had been glad. Instincts told her the other lady was there to make trouble. She braced herself for it.

"Well, you look the part of a blushing bride," Emily drawled, her lips curving into a sly smile.

Letitia stiffened, rising to her feet. "What do you want, Emily?"

Emily smirked, trailing her fingers along the edge of the vanity table. "To save you from a dreadful mistake, of course. I pity you, truly. You are about to wed a man who has deceived you in the most appalling way."

Letitia folded her arms, unwilling to give Emily the satisfaction of seeing her unease. "Nothing you say can ruin this day for me. I know you have always harbored ill will towards me because you are in love with Philip. Your bitterness does not concern me."

"Bitterness?" she let out a mocking laugh. "Oh, you poor, naïve thing. Do you truly believe Philip loves you? That he is marrying you for any reason other than your wealth?"

This again?

Letitia held her ground. "That is a lie. Philip has proven himself by relinquishing any claim to my fortune and even his title. He pursued me, even to the countryside, for my heart, not my inheritance."

Emily rolled her eyes. "How charmingly naïve. Tell me, Letitia, why would a man with vast finances tell you he is impoverished?"

Letitia frowned. "What do you mean?"

Emily tsked her tongue. "Have you never noticed the expensive clothes and jewelry Philip adorns himself with?"

"So?" She had noticed and even admired him for it.

"Does a supposed poor man dress so affluently?" she questioned with saccharine sweetness. "Let us not even talk about how he had his ducal carriage refurbished to his taste. I heard it gulped thousands of pounds. What about his—"

"Enough of this nonsense," Letitia snapped, though a sliver of doubt began to creep in. "If, as you say, he is wealthy, then he has no need for my wealth."

Emily shook her head. "Then you do not wonder why he lied to you in the first place? Why he kept his wealth in the dark? He amassed a sizeable inheritance from his grandfather and expanded it to become the wealthy man he is today."

Letitia struggled to keep her face impassive. Had she not suspected that Philip kept something from her when he told her how he came about inheriting the ducal title? Why had he not told her he was rich? She remembered he kept telling her he did not need her money... shouldn't he also have mentioned he was wealthy in his own right? Why hide it? And why had he initially pretended to be poor?

"Anyway, recent rumor has it that he is no longer as financially stable as he used to be. Two of his cargo ships are rumored to have capsized. He is in financial straits, and marrying you is his way out."

"If that is the case, why did he come after me? Why did he renounce everything if he is truly in dire need of my fortune?" she pointed out to the bitter woman.

Emily merely laughed. "Because there was a clause in your grandfather's will, you dimwit. He could not inherit it without your approval. And the only way to get it was to declare a fake love for you and then marriage to keep you sweet."

Letitia shook her head, refusing to accept the harsh words. "But there was no need for him to have done that when I was supposedly ousted as the heiress."

"Do not be gullible! Of course the solicitor did not believe that young man, particularly as Philip discovered he had been in cohort with someone to get rid of you. Why do you think he waited until it was confirmed that you were still a Barrington before he came after you with those tissues of lies?"

Letitia paled and turned away so Emily would not see the disbelief in her eyes.

Sweet Mary, what if it is true? She fought not to believe it, knowing Emily would do everything within her power for her not to be wed to Philip. Was this yet another obstacle for them to surmount?

She whirled around. "Why wait until today to tell me this? You have had four weeks to do this. Why now?"

"Because I only just found out. True, I am not happy about the marriage because I love Philip, but I have my pride. I will not be caught pining away for a man who loves money more than me. And the way Maria laughed in my face yesterday grated on my nerves. I have been fighting my conscience, and my mother told me to stay out of it. I wanted you to suffer when you discover that Philip married you only for your money, but then I decided to punish Philip also for casting me aside for you because of riches! I will not see him satisfied with your money at the end of the day!"

Letitia glared at her, wondering what to accept as true. She wished there was a way she could get to Philip with all these allegations so he could defend himself and put her worry to rest.

Emily pulled a folded paper from her reticule and held it out. "Perhaps you will believe your own eyes. Here is the evidence of his duplicity. This is a pact signed by Philip, Aunt Catherine, and others after your grandfather's will was read. They all conspired to drive you away and to secure your fortune for themselves."

Letitia's hands shook as she took the paper. The note read that they would do whatever it took to make sure the inheritance returned to the family and oust whoever the heiress was when found. The bold signatures at the bottom were unmistakable. Philip's name stared back at her like a betrayal carved in ink.

"You see?" Emily said, her tone almost pitying. "Philip is not the man you think he is."

"Even if this were true," Letitia refuted, "perhaps he had a change of heart. Mayhap he fell in love with me and was no longer a part of the wicked plot. I mean, why would he send Aunt Catherine and Maria packing? He caught them scheming against me. They despise each other right now. They are not even in support of our marriage."

Emily's laughter was bitter. "A convenient charade, is it not? You were the only one foolish enough to believe it. The farce was meant for you to trust Philip explicitly. They have been laughing their heads off at you. Maria told me so yesterday."

Letitia's heart screamed with denial. "You are lying! Philip loves me. He would not betray me this way."

"Believe what you will," Emily said with a shrug. "I only came to spare you the humiliation and to take revenge on him and his calculating family. The rest is up to you."

With that, Emily swept from the room, leaving Letitia alone with the damning document in her hands. What would she do? Dare she make the same mistake Philip did by believing Emily without hearing him out first? Accepting with face value the incriminating evidence against him?

Moments later, Aunt Helen and Frances returned. "Someone wanted us out of the room," Frances said angrily. "Mrs. Trowbridge did not request to see me, neither did our neighbors come."

Their expressions turned to concern as they saw Letitia's pale face.

"What has happened?" Aunt Helen demanded, hurrying to her side.

Letitia handed her the paper. "Emily said Philip... Philip has been lying to me. That he is marrying me for my fortune."

Aunt Helen's eyebrows knitted in confusion as she scanned the document. "This cannot be true. Philip loves you. He has shown it time and again."

Frances, however, looked troubled.

"What is it?" her mother asked.

Frances lowered her gaze. "I am sorry, Lettie. Before I entered the drawing room to her summons, I overheard Mrs. Trowbridge speaking with a relative about whether to tell you the truth. She seemed... uncertain."

Letitia's heart leapt to her throat. "Uncertain about what?"

Frances bit her lower lip and sighed. "About telling you about the pact, and that Philip is in cohort with Aunt Catherine and Maria."

Letitia's heart sank further as her world crumbled around her. "But she told me to pursue my feelings with Philip."

"Apparently, she only just found out the truth."

Tears smarted in Letitia's eyes as the truth dawned on her. "I cannot marry Philip."

Chapter 24: Philip

"Where is she?"

The atmosphere in the vestibule of St. James's Church grew heavier with every passing moment. Philip paced the length of the room, his polished shoes resounding against the stone floor. His hands clenched and unclenched at his sides, and the crisp folds of his sky-blue morning coat bore the evidence of his frustration. Thirty minutes! Thirty minutes late and still no sign of Letitia.

The murmurs from the congregation seeped through the heavy oak doors of the church, growing louder with each second. His stomach coiled as he imagined their pitying stares and speculative whispers.

Something must have happened. She will not do this to me. Will she?

"Philip, you are wearing a hole in the floor," James mentioned worriedly from his position against the wall, his face catching the light filtering through the arched windows. "Give her time. Women always take longer to prepare for such grand occasions."

"This is not a matter of a misplaced bonnet!" Philip snapped, running a hand through his hair, already disheveled from his relentless pacing and raking through. "Something is wrong. I can feel it."

James exchanged a glance with their younger brother, who straightened from his slouched position by the door.

"Do you want me to go to the Barrington townhouse to see what is keeping her?" Charles offered, already shrugging on his overcoat.

Philip halted for a moment, his pride warring with his fear. Finally, he nodded. "Go. And be quick about it."

Charles left quickly, and Philip resumed his pacing, his mind twirling with possibilities. His instincts told him this was not a simple delay. He recognized that he had made a grave mistake in not finding Andrew before the wedding. The former investigator's cryptic denials about the identity of his employer, even while in the custody of the authorities, had left too many loose ends.

"What if Aunt Catherine—" Philip began, but James cut him off.

"Do not let your mind run wild," James stated firmly. "Letitia loves you. Whatever this is, it will be resolved."

Philip wanted to believe him, but the knot in his stomach tightened with every tick of the clock. He had thought the worst was behind them. Letitia had forgiven him for his initial doubts, and they had spent weeks planning this day together. They had even spent a splendid day together the previous day and had both stated how they looked forward to being joined in holy matrimony. How could everything be ruined now?

The creak of the vestibule door interrupted his thoughts, and he turned to see Charles striding back in, and the look in his eyes was a blend of anger and regret. Philip's heart missed a beat as he feared the very worst had happened.

"Well?" he demanded sharply.

Charles paled and glanced at James before he spoke. "Aunt Helen sent word. Letitia has changed her mind about marrying you."

For a moment, Philip could only stare at him. Then the words sank in, and a surge of rage and despair coursed through him.

"Changed her mind?" he repeated with disbelief. "Just like that? With no explanation?"

Charles shook his head. "I was not offered any."

"That is absurd! She would not do this unless someone—" He stopped with his eyes darkening like a storm cloud. "Aunt Catherine and Maria! They must have got to her. Filled her head with lies. I should have followed my instincts by having them watched."

James drew abreast, placing a hand on his shoulder. "Philip, let us handle this while you—"

"No," Philip said, shaking him off. "I will speak to her myself. This nonsense ends now. Stall the crowd. Letitia will become my wife today, whether our devious cousins like it or not!"

Ignoring their protests, he stormed out of the church and climbed into his carriage. His heart pounded as the wheels rattled over the cobbled streets.

What could they have possibly told Letitia for her to renege on her promise to marry him? Did she have so little faith in him? He thought he had done everything possible for her to know how much he loved her. Apparently, it had not been enough for her to take this course of action without first seeking him out.

By the time they arrived at the Barrington townhouse, his fury had reached a boiling point.

Forbes, the ever-composed butler, opened the door with a bow. "Your Grace—"

"Where is she?" Philip demanded, brushing past him.

Forbes winced. "Lady Letitia has requested not to be disturbed."

Philip glared at him. "I will not leave until I speak to her."

He did not wait for a response before striding up the grand staircase two steps at a time. The door to Letitia's room stood ajar, and his heart twisted at the sight of her sitting by the window, her shoulders slumped. Aunt Helen and Frances flanked her, their faces reflecting worry. Letitia's eyes were red and swollen, evidence of tears he had not been there to comfort.

After a brief knock, he strode into the room. They all turned to look at him, wide-eyed.

"Aunt Helen, Frances, leave us," he commanded curtly.

Aunt Helen opened her mouth to protest, but one look at his face silenced her. With a hesitant glance at Letitia, she and Frances filed out of the room.

"Letitia," Philip began, ambling toward her with purposeful strides.

She rose and turned to face him with an icy look. "What are you doing here? I told Forbes I did not wish to see you."

Her tone was a dagger to his chest. He took a steadying breath and released it slowly to rein in his anger. "I came to find out why you no longer wish to marry me. What has changed?"

Her lips flattened into a thin line. "What has changed, *Your Grace*, is that I have learned the truth. You lied to me. About everything."

Just as I feared!

He frowned. "What lies? Who has been filling your head with nonsense?"

"It does not matter who told me," she answered with disdain. "What matters is that I know. You are not a poor man as you claimed, and you made a pact with your family to get rid of me. You only pursued me for my money."

He stiffened. "Letitia, that is not true. Yes, I am wealthy, which shows I never needed your money. And as for this so-called pact—"

"Do not deny it!" she interrupted. She snatched a sheet of paper from the table and thrust it at him. "Explain this, then."

He took the document, perused its contents and the signatures at the bottom. His stomach sank as he recognized his name alongside Aunt Catherine's and Maria's.

Indeed, it is their doing! Blasted cousins set to make me unhappy for material gains!

"This is a fabrication," he announced with anger. "Yes, there was an agreement, but not like this. Before I met you and fell in love with you, our family sought to ensure the heiress was worthy of the Barringtons' name and wealth. But when I realized their intentions went far beyond that—when I saw they meant to sabotage you—I refused to be part of it. That is why I am estranged from Aunt Catherine and Maria."

She scoffed in an unladylike fashion. "And I am to believe you knew nothing of the clause in my grandfather's will? That I must consent before you can take my wealth?"

His frown deepened. "What clause? I have heard no such thing."

She shook her head, a bitter laugh escaping her lips. "You expect me to believe you are innocent? That you had no hand in deceiving me?"

"Yes. Because it is the truth. I love you, Letitia."

She shook her head as if trying to erase his words. "Now I know why you were in such a hurry to marry me. Because you did not want me to discover the truth of your duplicity."

He jerked his head as if she had struck him. Coldly, he told her, "I was in a haste to marry you because I could not bear to be apart from you. Because I love you so much, I wanted to make you my wife and protect you from the cruelty of our family. Not because of your money."

For a moment, he thought he saw indecision in her eyes and hope rose inside him that he was finally getting through to her. But then, her eyes turned chilly like cold emeralds.

"What about your capsized ships? Can you deny that you are not in financial constraints?"

His hands balled into fists at her continued accusation. "I might have encountered a problem with my shipments, but that has nothing to do with your blasted money!" He raked his fingers through his hair with exasperation. "Can you not see, my love, that they are trying to draw us apart? To see that we are not happy together simply because I thwarted their plans?"

"This has nothing to do with our family, who I know you are in cohort with, by the way. The purported estrangement is just a travesty, is it not?"

He groaned. "Who fed you all these lies? Can you not see that you are allowing them to win? To succeed in placing a seed of discord between us?"

She shook her head again. "You have said enough. I cannot trust you again. You have lied to me time and time again. If you had told me you were wealthy, perhaps..." She placed a hand to her trembling lips as if holding back a sob. His heart wrenched at the sight, but she put up a hand when he reached for her. "I am sorry I cannot marry you. I will not be made a fool of again. What kind of marriage would we have without trust?"

Something in Philip's heart shattered at her words. He drew himself up, his face like granite.

"Very well." His voice was devoid of emotion. "Perhaps it is a blessing in disguise that this wedding will not proceed. If you cannot trust me after all I have done to prove my love, then we have no future together. 'Tis obvious you will always think of me as a fortune hunter." He shook his head. "Mayhap I was wrong about you. You are a Barrington, after all. I can see now that you deserve your relatives, from whom I have tried to protect you."

He turned on his heel, striding towards the door. Pausing on the threshold, he glanced back at her.

"May mistrust bring you the love and happiness I would have given you," he said quietly. Then he walked away, leaving his heart behind in the room.

Chapter 25: Letitia

Two days later, Letitia sat on the edge of her bed, her hands grasping a handkerchief already damp with her tears. Her room felt like a prison cell as she could not bear to go out for fear of the stares and whispers she was certain the *ton* would subject her to. Only an occasional sniffle she could not suppress broke the silence.

Her thoughts spiraled between regret and confusion. Have I been too hasty? she wondered for the hundredth time. Every recollection of Philip's stormy departure made her chest ache. She had thought herself strong in rejecting him, in protecting herself from deceit, but all she had done was feel the sharp sting of loss.

The door opened, and Aunt Catherine swept in, her sharp eyes glinting like the blade of a dagger. Dressed faultlessly in a deep green gown, her bonnet adorned with a matching feather, she carried herself with the air of someone who always had the last word.

"Well, well," her aunt said, her lips curving into a shrill smile. "How the mighty have fallen." She made a show of surveying Letitia's blotchy face and disheveled hair, shaking her head in mock dismay.

Letitia straightened her spine, though her unsteady hands betrayed her inner turmoil. "What do you want, Aunt?"

"To deliver the consequences of your actions," Aunt Catherine said, sinking into the window seat. "You have not only broken a man's heart but made a mockery of him before all of England. Philip Henshaw, the Duke of Wynthorpe—a laughingstock! And all because of your caprice."

Letitia's stomach twisted. "I—I did not mean to cause him humiliation."

"Oh, did you not?" the older woman curved an eyebrow. "You left him standing at the altar! That man, foolish as he may be, loved you. He took your side against his family—against me, even—and you repaid him by shattering his dignity. Bravo, Letitia, truly."

Her aunt's words struck like barbs. "You were the one who said he would never marry me for love," Letitia whispered brokenly.

Aunt Catherine shook her head. "And yet he proved me wrong, did he not? He turned his back on his inheritance for you. You made him a pauper in the eyes of society, and for what? Your cursed wealth? And now we face a scandal, the very first attached to the family name, because of you." She rose, smoothing her skirts with a practiced hand. "You have proven yourself a fool, but not half as much as Philip for loving you. A pity, truly."

The door closed sharply behind her, leaving Letitia in stunned silence. She crumpled forward, tears spilling anew. She wished her grandfather had never found out about her, and that she had continued living peacefully in the countryside, blissfully unaware of her roots. Again, she wondered if she had made a terrible mistake by listening to Emily. Philip's countenance had made her think she was wrong, but she had feared that she was allowing her heart to do the talking instead of her brain. She was no longer so sure she had made the right decision—she loved Philip so much and missed him terribly. And now Aunt Catherine, who was supposedly in cahoots with Philip, had called her a fool for breaking his heart.

Or is it just a ploy for me to accept him back, marry him, and then they will get their hands on my inheritance? A tiny voice asked. She did not know what to think anymore.

Had Aunt Catherine indeed spoken the truth? She thought of Philip's anguished face, his vehement words, and his wounded pride. Had she let fear and doubt poison everything they could have had together?

By the time Frances entered her room that afternoon, Letitia's mind was a turbulent sea of indecision. Frances's kind brown eyes were filled with concern as she sat beside her cousin.

"You look dreadful, Lettie," she said gently, brushing back a strand of Letitia's hair.

"Thank you for that astute observation," Letitia replied with a weak smile.

Frances clasped her hands. "Come now, you cannot wallow in this forever. Have you considered going back to Brookstone for a while? You were happy there."

"Running away will not change what I have done," Letitia murmured. "I hurt him, Fran. He will never forgive me."

"You do not know that. If you truly believe you made a mistake, perhaps it is not too late to set things right."

Letitia's heart squeezed at the thought. She could not bear the idea of living without Philip, yet her fear of rejection held her back.

She spent the night tossing and turning, her mind replaying every moment of their tumultuous relationship.

***

The following evening found Letitia in the garden, a serene place for her riotous thoughts. She wandered aimlessly, her pink gown fluttering in the breeze.

Frances had mentioned Brookstone again during breakfast, which she'd had no appetite for, urging her to leave the scandal behind. The idea had merit, but it also felt like surrender. Nonetheless, she had agreed to go. Perhaps a change of setting would give her a clearer mind. But would it? Would she not see Philip wherever she went in the village, remembering when he was there?

She stared at a cluster of red roses, wondering if she would ever feel as vibrant again. That morning she had gone for a walk, hoping to clear her head, but had hurried back when she kept receiving stares from ladies who talked behind their handkerchiefs and fans as she walked past. The scandal her rejection caused had indeed taken root. She cringed as she thought of what Philip would be going through. She hoped he could withstand the wagging tongues unlike her, who intended to flee the city. She could only hope she would find a respite in Brookstone.

A familiar voice interrupted her reverie.

"Your Grace!" she heard Emily say with excitement.

Letitia's heart leapt. Philip! Without thinking, she turned and hurried towards the side door leading to the foyer. Her heart pounded as she imagined his face that she had missed so much. Was he there to make her listen to him again? She definitely would with every fiber of her being.

But it was not Philip she found. Standing in the foyer was James, tall and commanding in a charcoal-grey frock coat. Emily stood beside him, beaming from ear to ear. Disappointment wafted through Letitia.

"Your Grace, will you join us for dinner?" Emily requested with a coy smile.

"Your Grace?" Letitia questioned with a frown.

James turned with a somber expression. "Lady Letitia," he greeted, bowing slightly.

"Did Emily just call you Your Grace?" she asked sharply, the question escaping before she could temper her tone.

"Yes. I came to deliver the news," he replied quietly. "Philip has renounced the title and everything attached to it. As of an hour ago, I am the Duke of Wynthorpe."

Letitia gasped, her hand flying to her mouth. "He renounced it?"

James nodded. "He wanted no part of it. I thought this household should know before the word gets out, although I am sure Philip will blacken my eyes if he knows I am here telling *you* this."

Letitia's knees wobbled, and she clutched the banister for support. "Why would he do such a thing?"

"Perhaps *you* should ask him," James said pointedly. "If you can manage to stop doubting him for long enough to listen."

His words stung, but Letitia could not argue.

Dear God, I have made a dreadful mistake.

Her face crumbled and with a sob she could not suppress, she lifted the skirts of her gown and hurried up the stairs, her heart heavy with regret.

Aunt Helen and Frances were waiting for her in her room, their worried faces softening when they saw her.

"What is the matter, dear child?" Aunt Helen asked.

Letitia sank onto the chaise longue, trembling with sobs as she relayed what James had told her.

"He told me time and time again that the title and the money meant nothing to him, but I allowed the people who do not want us to be together to fill my head with lies. How can I claim to love him when I do not trust him and I hurt him repeatedly?"

Aunt Helen pulled her into a tight embrace. "'Tis not your fault, my dear. The evidence was stacked against him. It does not mean you do not love him. You are very young and bound to make mistakes as you have lived a sheltered life."

"But you, in your wisdom, told me not to listen to them but him. I did not listen. I allowed my fears to becloud my judgment."

"But I also told you not to trust him."

"In the beginning. You got to know him and knew he was to be trusted. I knew I could trust him when he came to Brookstone, but I do not know why I did not listen to him when he told me our family meant to tear us apart."

Aunt Helen sighed. "Then you know what you must do."

"I was such a fool," Letitia whispered. "How could I have doubted him? I love him so much."

Frances squeezed her hand. "Then tell him that. It is not too late, Lettie. You can still make amends."

Letitia nodded, hope rising in her chest. "I will go to him."

Her aunt shook her head. "Leave it for the morrow. 'Tis too late to call on him now."

The night stretched endlessly before Letitia, every passing hour filled with anticipation and dread. She feared Philip would not listen to her because not only had she broken his heart; she had hurt his pride as well.

I will beg him on my knees if I have to.

The next morning, Letitia stood before her mirror, her fingers shaking as she adjusted her bonnet. She took a deep breath, steeling herself for what lay ahead. As she descended the stairs with Frances, a maid approached with a note in hand.

"A message for you, my lady."

Letitia unfolded the note, and her eyes widened as she read the familiar scrawl.

Letitia, my love,Meet me at my townhouse. There is much to discuss.Philip.

Her heart soared. She clutched the note to her chest, a smile breaking through her anxiety.

"I must go posthaste," she said happily.

Frances followed her to the door. "Shall I accompany you?"

"No. This is something I must do alone."

She climbed into the waiting carriage, hope blooming within her as it carried her towards the man she would forever love and learn to trust.

Chapter 26: Philip

Philip sat at the breakfast table, staring blankly at the plate of eggs and ham before him. For days, hHis appetite had been as absent as his peace of mind. Across the table, his brothers were deep in conversation about a subject he would rather not discuss—Letitia.

"I dare say you have made a thorough mess of this, Philip," Charles declared, his tone as sharp as the butter knife he brandished. "If it were me, I would have hauled her to the church, locked the doors, and made sure we were married before I explained myself. A duchess has little room to argue once the deed is done."

James smirked and shook his head. "And that, dear brother, is why you will never marry. Compulsion is hardly the way to a woman's heart. If I were in Philip's position, I would have explained everything to her calmly and refused to leave her presence until she saw sense. Trust is the foundation of any relationship, and Philip shattered hers."

A scowl darkened Philip's features. He set down his teacup with deliberate care. "Are you quite finished?"

"No," James said with maddening calmness. "You have been utterly miserable without her, Philip. It is painful to watch, frankly. You lied to her about your wealth, and worse, you let our odious cousins sway your judgment when she first arrived, and initially refused to take her side when they accused her of not being the heiress. Do you truly not understand why she does not trust you?"

Charles groaned. "I still say you should have taken my approach. Quick and decisive."

James ignored him and fixed Philip with a penetrating gaze. "She loves you, you know."

Philip snorted at his brother's allusion. Wary of the conversation, he pushed back his chair abruptly, the legs scraping against the wooden floor. "I have no intention of listening further. Thankfully, I will be away from London before the end of the week."

Charles raised a brow. "Away? Where could you possibly be going?"

"The West Indies," Philip replied coolly. "There are business opportunities I must attend to now that I am no longer a duke."

James's teacup froze halfway to his mouth. "The West Indies? Have you lost your senses? You cannot leave, not when Letitia—"

Philip cut him off angrily. "What would you have me do, James? Beg her forgiveness on bended knee? She made her choice. She does not trust me, and I cannot fault her for it. As she wishes to live her life without me, I will not stand in her way."

They had no idea the anguish that plagued him at her distrust and rejection. He had to leave, for he could not bear the ache anymore, knowing they were in the same city and could not be together because of her uncertainties about him.

James grunted. "With all due respect, Philip, do not be a fool. Letitia realized her mistake the moment I told her you had renounced the title. After a horrific look on her face which, to me, meant that she grasped her folly about you, she ran upstairs sobbing. Sobbing. Does that sound like a woman indifferent to you?"

Philip stilled. "She… sobbed?"

"She did," James confirmed. "She is miserable without you, just as you are without her. Are you truly willing to throw away everything—your love, your happiness—just to spare your pride?"

Philip's heart squeezed painfully. He looked away, his fingers tightening around the edge of the table. "And what of her distrust? Her refusal to believe in me when it mattered most?"

"She was frightened," James reminded gently. "You lied to her, Philip. You must understand that her doubt stemmed from your own actions."

Try as he might, he could not deny that his reaction to her when they first met until he fell in love with her did not make him look trustworthy. But he had done everything within his power to make her look beyond the obnoxious person he was to her before he got to know her.

James sighed. "Frances told me she is considering retreating to the countryside for good and giving up the Barrington name and her inheritance."

Philip jerked with mortification.

"She cannot endure London and its scandal anymore. Are you truly going to let her slip away because of your pride?"

Anger burned inside him at the news that Letitia planned to give it all up. So, she was willing to throw away everything so that Aunt Catherine and Maria would win despite everything they had done to them? Never! He would not let her. After the heartache their family had caused them, he would make sure they did not see a penny of the money.

Finally, Philip nodded. "I will speak with her."

Charles clapped his hands with glee. "At last, some sense!"

"I promise nothing," Philip warned. "If she does not wish to see me—"

"Then you will convince her otherwise," James interrupted with a grin. "Now go, before she flees to the countryside and Charles and I lose such a beautiful and sweet sister-in-law for good."

Philip wasted no time. He called for his coat and hat, then set off for the Barrington townhouse with determination and rage simmering beneath his calm exterior. After listening to his brothers for days on end, he grudgingly understood why she would not trust him after all that happened. Perhaps, if she was willing, they could both live quietly, away from all the drama of the inheritance and title. That was if she still loved him… because he very much still loved her, although he was still hurt that she did not trust him.

When he arrived, Aunt Helen and Frances greeted him in the drawing room, their faces lighting up at the sight of him.

"Philip!" Frances exclaimed with delight. "My! You must be eager to see Letitia. I am afraid she already departed."

"Departed?" he repeated, frowning. Then his heart missed a beat. "To Brookstone?"

Aunt Helen frowned. "No. To your residence. She received your note and left to see you not an hour ago."

"My note?" His frown deepened. "I sent no such note."

The color drained from Frances's face. "You… did not?"

"No." A chill settled over Philip's chest. "What did the note say?"

"To go to your townhouse to discuss," Frances answered with alarm. "She was eager to speak with you."

Philip turned on his heel without another word. If he had not sent the note, then who had? And what was their purpose in luring Letitia away?

By the time he reached his townhouse, his chest was heaving, and his hands quivered with barely suppressed panic. He burst through the door, startling his butler.

"Your Grace!" the man exclaimed.

"Where is she?" Philip demanded. "Lady Letitia... has she arrived?"

The butler shook his head. "No, Your Grace. There has been no sign of her."

Philip's pulse raced. Fear gripped him like a vise as he turned and strode back out into the street. There was only one person who might have orchestrated such a scheme.

Aunt Catherine!

His carriage rolled to a halt outside the townhouse, where Aunt Catherine was still residing and he stormed inside, ignoring the protests of the butler. He found her in the drawing room, sipping tea with her usual air of superiority.

"Philip," she drawled, raising an eyebrow. "What an unexpected visit."

"Where is she?" he bellowed.

She blinked. "Who?"

"Do not play coy with me," he snapped. "Where is Letitia? What have you done to her?"

She set her teacup down with a sigh. "I have no idea what you are blathering about. Letitia is not here, nor do I know where she is."

"You sent a false note to lure her away," he accused with a savage bite. "Do not deny it."

Her gaze hardened. "I swear on my late father's grave, I did no such thing. Believe me or do not, but I would not stoop so low."

Philip searched her face for any sign of deceit, but she appeared genuinely affronted. If not Aunt Catherine, then who?

"If anything happens to her, and I find out you had anything to do with it, you will not like what I will do to you!"

She gasped.

He turned and left, his mind a whirlwind of fear and fury. Letitia was missing, and the note that lured her away was a trap. But who had sent it and why?

Chapter 27: Letitia

The first thing Letitia noticed was the biting chill in the air. Her head throbbed painfully as she struggled to open her eyes. A dim, flickering light from a single candle illuminated the small, decrepit room. The wooden walls were rough and uneven, the floor covered in a thin layer of grime. The stench of dampness and decay hung heavily in the air, turning her stomach.

She tried to move but found her wrists bound behind her. Her arms ached, and the lovely dress she had chosen for her visit to Philip was now dirty and torn at the hem. She tried to think, to remember how she had ended up here.

The carriage!

She had entered it with her heart heavy with trepidation but eager to speak with Philip. The wheels had barely begun to turn when the carriage had lurched to a stop. Then came the sound of the door opening, a figure lunging in, and the suffocating smell of the cloth pressed against her face. After that, only darkness.

The creak of a door startled her. She blinked rapidly, focusing on the shadowy figure entering the room. Her breath caught as she recognized the face.

"Mrs. Trowbridge?"

The older woman closed the door behind her with deliberate care, her eyes cold and calculating. Clad in a plain brown cloak, her appearance was far from the genteel figure Letitia had always known. Mrs. Trowbridge pulled a chair from the corner and sat, her movements calm and unhurried.

"I see you are awake," she said with a voice devoid of warmth.

Letitia struggled against her bonds, glaring at the woman before her. "What is the meaning of this? Why have you brought me here? What have I done to deserve such treatment?"

The older woman's lips curled into a bitter smile. "What have you done? My dear, you had the misfortune of being born."

Letitia froze. "I do not understand."

She leaned back in her chair as her face darkened. "Of course, you do not. How could you? You, with your lovely features and your air of innocence. The very sight of you has been a thorn in my side for years."

"Years?" Letitia whispered, her confusion deepening.

"Allow me to enlighten you." She snarled, her voice dripping with derision. "Once upon a time, I was young and full of promise. I had a friend, Catherine, your aunt, and through her, I met Henry, your father."

Letitia swallowed thickly.

"I adored him," she continued, her eyes hardening. "We were close, closer than anyone suspected. I thought... I hoped... But then he met Clara, your mother." She spat the name like a curse.

A frown creased Letitia's forehead. "My parents... They were in love. They—"

"Do not speak of love to me!" she snapped, rising to her feet. "He betrayed me, cast me aside for that woman, that pauper. And what did I receive in return? Nothing but humiliation."

Letitia's throat tightened, but she forced herself to speak. "You... you cannot mean to harm me because of a grievance from years ago."

A harsh laugh burst from her throat. "Oh, my dear, you underestimate me. Fool that he was, not realizing my feelings for him, Henry told me everything and swore me to secrecy until he could tell his father, who had already cut off Catherine for marrying a commoner. What he did not know was that he was giving me ammunition for my plan." She tsked her tongue. "I tried to rid myself of Clara once before, but the foolish woman survived. When you were born, I vowed that neither of you would find happiness. I nearly succeeded in removing you as an infant, but the blasted maid betrayed me, and your wretched aunt spirited you away."

Letitia's eyes widened with horror. Mrs. Trowbridge was the one who had tried to do away with her, not her grandfather? Oh, how harshly she had judged the innocent man.

The older woman's gaze turned cruel. "I thought you were dead until I intercepted a letter from your Aunt Helen to Henry, informing him that you were still alive and she had taken you someplace safe. I seized every letter she sent to your father without his knowledge. I tried to find the both of you, but any time I was within arm's reach, she took you away as if she knew I was hot on her heels. And then the letters stopped coming." She smiled with satisfaction, then scowled. "I thought Henry would then turn to me for solace, but he did not. I watched as he wasted away, bereft of his wife and child. It was no less than he deserved."

Letitia's chest constricted as tears stung her eyes. "You... you were the reason my father never found us."

The image of her father, a man she had never known, suffering in silence, tore at her heart. She had thought he had not wanted to know her, but she had been wrong. Her heart twisted at the thought of the poor man who had died not knowing she was alive. And at the life she would have lived, knowing she had a father who would have loved her dearly.

Anger pulsated inside her. "You wicked witch! What do you want now? Have you not caused enough hurt and damage already?"

She sneered. "Mind your words, you twit. I have not even begun to enact my revenge for what your mother cost me. I had dreamt of becoming a duchess. I was not titled, but my father was a wealthy merchant. I had a huge dowry that would have made your grandfather overlook the fact that I was not from the upper class. But Clara took all that away from me," she spat with venom. Then she smiled coldly. "But I sought to remedy all that with my daughter."

"Emily," Letitia breathed.

Her expression turned calculating once more. "If I could not be a duchess, then my daughter would take that place. When I noticed she took a fancy to Philip, I encouraged the friendship, knowing she would worm her way into the heart of the man who was next in line to the dukedom. She was my hope, my revenge." Her face contorted into a frown. "But then the late duke's infernal stipulations ruined everything. And you—" She pointed a bony finger at Letitia. "You stood in the way."

Letitia could only glare at her as she tried to take in the wicked woman's revelations.

Her face twisted in an ugly frown. "I did not know your foolish father confided in your grandfather. I would have done everything possible to get rid of you." She gave her a wintry smile. "I had to do something or watch my plans go up in flames again. It was so easy to manipulate Catherine and Maria to hate you, given that they were already put out by the will. I did not come out bluntly to say they should sabotage you, but a carefully worded suggestion of you not fitting in or subtle words of them doing something about it and then telling them not to mind me sowed the seeds I needed." She frowned. "But it was not so easy with Philip. He never fell for my supposedly innocent suggestions. So, I tried using Emily to get to him, as they were friends, and he used to take her counsel, but that did not work either. You had bewitched him, and he was smitten!"

Anguish tore at Letitia at the memory of mistrusting Philip at every turn when he was the only one who had not fallen for the evil woman's gimmicks.

"So, I focused on Catherine and Maria to do my dirty work for me and make your life a living hell."

Looking confused, Letitia reminded her, "But you always stood up for me. You even advised me to pursue my feelings for Philip."

Mocking laughter erupted from the older woman's throat. "But of course! It was all a ruse. I did not want anyone pointing fingers at me. I had to look innocent in case things did not go as planned."

Letitia's body shook with anger. She felt terribly foolish for ever trusting her. "You manipulated everyone. You turned Aunt Catherine and Maria against me. You..." She faltered and bit back tears of frustration. "You sent Emily to me with that false pact and lies."

She smirked. "Very perceptive, my dear. It was all so easy. Catherine and Maria's resentment was a flame I merely had to fan. As for you, your lack of trust in others made you an easy target. Emily and I bided our time while you went prancing about as the happy bride-to-be. We waited until the morning of your wedding so you could not speak to

Philip, who would undoubtedly have been able to change your mind. It was so easy to get your aunt and cousin to exit your bedchamber, and to make sure Frances heard me speaking to a hired woman posing as a relative."

Letitia bowed her head with sorrow. Her failure to trust Philip had cost her dearly. "Philip was the only one who believed in me," she murmured.

Mrs Trowbridge's smile widened. "And yet you turned against him, just as I knew you would."

Letitia's head shot up, and her eyes gleamed with defiance. "What do you intend to do now? What purpose does kidnapping me serve? Everyone will be looking for me… including Philip as he sent for me."

The older woman's expression darkened once more. "You are an obstacle, Letitia. As long as you live, you threaten Emily's happiness. Philip is no longer the duke, which makes him useless. Emily will marry James, and the title and wealth of the family will be ours."

"You are mad!" Letitia seethed.

Mrs. Trowbridge's smile turned wicked. "Am I? I think not. I have planned this meticulously. And oh, my dear, you naïve little fool. Philip will not be looking for you. He will be too busy trying to get himself out of the hangman's noose."

Letitia frowned. "What do you mean?"

"I employed the services of a good forger, who forged the handwriting and signatures on the pact and replicated Philip's distinctive scrawl."

Letitia's heart skipped a beat. "The note is fake?"

"Precisely. I heard you finally believed he was innocent of all the accusations you threw against him and wanted to make amends. I could not allow that, not after all the new plans I had made when I got word that he relinquished the dukedom to James. By the time your body is found in a crate, poisoned, and ready to be shipped on Philip's vessel, he will be blamed. Paid witnesses will swear they saw him arguing with you in front of his townhouse. The shame of your rejection will be motive enough for society to condemn him."

Letitia's blood ran cold. "You cannot believe anyone would accept such a story. Everyone knows Philip cannot hurt a fly."

She chuckled, reaching into her cloak. She withdrew a small vial filled with a clear liquid. "Oh, my dear, I have thought of everything."

She moved to the table, uncorking the vial and pouring its contents into a tarnished silver goblet. A shiver of trepidation ran through Letitia's spine. She tugged desperately at her bonds as her eyes were transfixed on the goblet.

Mrs. Trowbridge turned to her with a malevolent gleam in her eyes. "It is time, my dear. Do not worry. It will be quick."

Letitia's pulse thundered in her ears as the older woman advanced with the goblet.

Chapter 28: Philip

Philip paced the length of the drawing room. He turned to Aunt Helen, who sat on a settee with Frances, both clutching handkerchiefs dampened with tears. The usually stately room felt stifling, its elegant décor failing to provide any semblance of comfort.

Frances sniffled, dabbing at her eyes. "What could have happened to her? She was so excited to go to you, so full of joy. And now—" Her voice broke, and she buried her face in her hands. "I should have gone with her."

Aunt Helen placed a quivering hand on her daughter's shoulder. "We must pray, Frances. The Lord will protect Letitia. He must."

Philip stilled, his hands curling into fists. "Prayers will not bring her back, Aunt Helen," he said brusquely. "We need action."

The three Bow Street Runners in the room exchanged uneasy glances, their presence adding little assurance. They had scoured the house and questioned the servants, and yet their investigation seemed no closer to yielding results.

"Has no one confessed anything yet?" Philip demanded with frustration. "Not a single servant saw or heard anything unusual?"

One of the runners, a tall man with a thin mustache, cleared his throat. "We questioned them thoroughly, Your Grace."

Philip did not bother correcting the man about no longer bearing the title.

"None have admitted to anything suspicious. They claim innocence."

"Innocence!" Philip's voice thundered through the room, and Aunt Helen flinched. "I am tempted to have them all arrested for negligence, at the very least."

He began pacing the room again, wondering what more he could do to find Letitia. Like a crazed man, he had ridden around the streets of London in search of her, to no avail. When he received word that the Bow Street Runners he had hired were in residence, he had hurried back, hoping to receive good news for them. To his disappointment, they, too, had sent their men in search of her, but it seemed as if she had disappeared into thin air after getting into the carriage. Even the conveyance had not been found. James and Charles were still out looking while he had two footmen watching the house where his cousins were staying.

Philip gritted his teeth. If only he had swallowed his bloody pride and sought her out these days past. Even though he had been hurt by her rejection, he should have tried to make her see sense and convinced her of his love, just like he had done when he left it all and went to Brookstone. And now she was nowhere to be found. If anything happened to her, he did not think he could bear it... or forgive himself.

Although he had told the women that their prayers were futile, he could not help praying for divine intervention.

Dear God, if you bring her back safely, I promise to be by her side always and make her trust me and love me again.

A tense silence filled the room until Forbes entered. His usual composed demeanor was somewhat frayed. "My lord," he announced hesitantly, "an old woman has arrived and insists on speaking with you. She claims it is urgent."

Philip frowned. "An old woman?"

Frances perked up, her tear-streaked face pinched with curiosity. "Perhaps she knows something, Philip. Did she give her name?"

Before Forbes could respond, the woman entered unbidden. She was hunched with age, her face deeply lined, and her grey hair tucked under a modest bonnet. Her worn shawl and threadbare gown betrayed a life of poverty.

Philip gasped and stared at the woman he and Letitia had met in Westridge a short while ago. The maid who had served Lady Clara. Why did she look much older than when they last saw her?

Aunt Helen drew in a ragged breath, rising to her feet. "Lucy!"

The name struck like a thunderclap. Philip's gaze snapped to Aunt Helen, who looked as though she had seen a ghost. He nodded. Of course, she would know the old woman since she had lived in that house in Westridge with her sister.

"This... this is the maid who tried to kill Letitia as a baby!" Aunt Helen exclaimed.

Frances recoiled. "What?"

Philip froze and glared at Lucy. "You conveniently left out that bit of information when Letitia and I met you in Westridge."

Lucy wrung her hands, her eyes darting nervously around the room. "Aye, it is true, Your Grace. I was too ashamed to tell you. But I am here to make amends. I could not stay silent any longer."

Philip crossed the room in two strides, his imposing figure towering over the frail woman. "What is the meaning of this?" he demanded. "Why now, after all these years?"

Lucy flinched but stood her ground. "I could not live with the guilt any longer."

Aunt Helen glared at her. "You mean the guilt of attempting to murder an innocent child?"

Lucy shook her head vehemently. "I would not have done it! I swear it. Yes, I was paid to, but I could not bring myself to harm her. I fled instead and have been in hiding all these years. But when my sister, who stayed in the house as a maid, fell terribly sick with no one to cater for her, I had to return. She died after tending to her for months. After her demise, I wanted to leave again, but I realized the cottage was going to ruin as no one lived there. My sister had told me no one ever came calling since I ran away, and after you took the baby and left. So, I decided to stay and tend to it. Your Grace, when you and Lady Letitia came to the house, I desperately wanted to tell you everything, but I was afraid of what you would do to me. After you departed, I knew I had to do something. I had to say the truth, no matter the consequences. I would have been here earlier, but I fell ill on the way to London and was bedridden for a while until I regained strength to come here, seeking to do the right thing by my late lady and her daughter."

Philip's eyes narrowed. "Who gave the order?"

The room held its collective breath. Lucy hesitated, her gaze shifting to the Bow Street Runners, then to the door as though considering escape.

"If, as you say, you are here to make amends, then you must tell us who paid you to take the life of an innocent child," he said in between clenched teeth.

The woman quaked before him, but he was not moved. Letitia's life was in danger. Everything in him told him who tried to kill her twenty years ago was the same person who had abducted her.

"Please tell us," Frances begged. "Letitia is missing!"

Lucy raised stunned eyes to hers. "What?"

"You will tell us," Philip commanded coldly, "or you will find yourself in Newgate before the hour is out."

One of the runners, a burly man with a scar across his cheek, stepped forward. "Madam, if you have information pertinent to Lady Letitia's disappearance, you are obliged to share it. If not, the consequences will be severe."

Lucy swallowed hard. "I... I was threatened," she stammered. "The person said they would kill me if I ever spoke of it. I have lived in fear all these years."

Frances let out a soft sob, and her mother gripped her hand.

Philip's hands fisted at his sides as fury gushed through him. "In fear? What about Letitia? She grew up not knowing her true identity!"

Lucy shook her head, tears flooding her wrinkled face. "I was naïve and frightened. I did not know what to do. I fled, thinking the child would be safe with her aunt who caught me. I knew nothing more about the matter until you and Lady Letitia came. I am sorry. So very sorry."

"Enough dillydallying!" Philip barked, his patience worn thin. "Who was it?"

Lucy's lips trembled as she whispered, "I did not know her name initially until the curricle driver called her to tell her they had to leave because it was getting dark."

"Who?" Philip growled.

"Mrs. Trowbridge."

Chapter 29: Letitia

Letitia quivered like a leaf in the wind as she sat in the dimly lit chamber, her heart pounding like a war drum. Mrs. Trowbridge loomed before her, her hair escaped from its pins in wild tendrils, and her eyes gleamed with a dangerous fervor.

"You must understand," she hissed, clutching the goblet. "This is for the greater good. You were never meant to exist. Your mother stole everything that should have belonged to me."

Letitia struggled to her feet and took a cautious step back, her skirts brushing against the edge of a rickety wooden table. "You are mad. This vendetta of yours has consumed you. I have no intention of standing in your daughter's way. I planned to return to the countryside and forsake everything."

Her laugh was sharp, devoid of mirth. "You expect me to believe that? No, Letitia. As long as you breathe, you are a threat to Emily's future. And I cannot allow that."

Letitia inhaled sharply as the older woman advanced. The acrid smell of the goblet's contents reached her nose, making her stomach churn.

"Stay away from me," Letitia warned.

Mrs. Trowbridge shook her head with a look of twisted pity. "It is nothing personal, my dear. It is simply necessity."

As the woman lunged forward, Letitia darted to the side, her silk gown snagging on the splintered chair. She tugged herself free and tried to make for the door, but Mrs. Trowbridge was surprisingly swift in blocking her path.

"You will not escape," she snarled, pulling a dagger from the folds of her dress. The blade glinted in the candlelight, and Letitia's face paled.

"Have you no shred of humanity left?" Letitia cried. "You would kill me in cold blood?"

Mrs. Trowbridge's lip curled. "Do not mistake this for a lack of heart. It pains me to do this because you are actually a sweet lady, but 'tis for the best."

Letitia's mind twirled as she tried to come up with a smart way to get out of the dire situation. She needed to stall. She could not bear not to see Philip ever again and not tell him how much she loved him. And dear God, he could not be framed for her death. "If you truly believe that, then why are you trying to kill me yourself when you did not do it twenty years ago? Why now?"

The question seemed to strike a nerve. She paused. "Because I cannot trust others to do what needs to be done. Clearly, my earlier attempts failed, thanks to that spineless maid."

Letitia seized the opportunity to edge closer to the door. "And yet here I stand. Does that not tell you something? Perhaps fate has other plans."

Her eyes hardened. "Fate does not concern itself with the likes of us." She lunged with the dagger aimed at Letitia's throat. Letitia screamed. Just then, the door burst open with a thunderous crash, splinters flying, and hit Mrs Trowbridge in the face. She staggered back with shock.

"Letitia!" Philip's voice rang out like salvation itself. He stormed into the room, his tall frame cutting a striking figure. His cravat was loosened, and his coat hung open, revealing his waistcoat. Behind him, the Bow Street Runners poured in.

"Philip, be careful!" Letitia cried, retreating as Philip moved swiftly between her and Mrs. Trowbridge.

Mrs. Trowbridge screamed, a sound that sent shivers down Letitia's spine. "She must die! She must!" The woman's shriek was feral, her once-smug facade now utterly shattered. "She will ruin everything!"

One of the Bow Street Runners grabbed her arm, wrenching the dagger from her grasp. She struggled like a wild animal, kicking and spitting. "You do not understand! It is for my daughter! For her future!"

"Take her away," Philip instructed shortly.

As the runners dragged Mrs. Trowbridge from the room, she continued to scream. "You are all fools! She is a curse! She will destroy us all like she destroyed my daughter and me!"

Silence descended, broken only by Letitia's ragged breathing after they left. Philip turned to her, and with the dagger the runner handed to him before he left he cut her bonds loose. Letitia winced as she flexed her hands, staring at the angry red lines marking her wrists.

Philip's eyes earnestly searched her face. "Are you hurt, my love?"

She shook her head, though her knees threatened to buckle. "No, but—" Her voice faltered, and before she could say more, he dipped and swung her into his arms. He carried her out of the room, down a narrow corridor, and through the front door. She dimmed her eyes at the brightness of the sun and lowered her gaze after noting they were surrounded by grassland and were probably in the outskirts of London. She did not even lift her head when Philip gently placed her on the plush leather seat of his ducal carriage. Shame for the poor way she had treated him coursed through her.

"My love, are you sure you are all right? She did not harm you, did she?"

His softly spoken words were her undoing. She burst into tears with pent up relief from her ordeal. She was not dead, and Philip was right there with her.

"Oh, my darling. Thank God you are safe," he murmured gruffly as he tenderly pulled her into his arms once more. "I thought I had lost you. In all my twenty-seven years on earth, I have never been so scared. What would I have done if we had not come at that moment?"

She clung to him, sobbing while he stroked her hair softly, muttering words of love and comfort until she was spent. Her hands fisted in the fabric of his waistcoat. "Mrs. Trowbridge," she whispered in a hoarse voice, "she was behind everything from the onset. She told me... she told me how she orchestrated it all."

He pulled back just enough to look into her eyes. "She will never harm you again. I swear it."

She nodded without a shred of doubt. "I am so sorry, Philip. I should have believed you. I should have trusted you."

He brushed a strand of hair from her face. "None of that matters now. What matters is that you are safe."

"How did you find me?" She smiled through her tears, still not believing he was there with her... and still loved her.

Philip's lips twitched into a faint smile. "It was the old woman, Lucy. She came forward and told us everything. She revealed that Mrs.

Trowbridge was behind the attempt on your life as a child. When we could not find you, we pressed Emily. She confessed to her part in the scheme, though she claimed she did it out of misguided love for me and had no idea her mother had planned to kidnap you. She also revealed which servants were working for her mother. Upon questioning them, we learned from the footman who drove the carriage where you had been taken."

Her eyes dimmed with sadness. "I never knew Emily hated me so much."

His face turned grim. "She does foolishly, fueled by her cruel mother. She claimed ignorance of her mother's more... violent intentions, though I am not inclined to believe her entirely."

She shook her head. "And the servants?"

"Forbes, two footmen, and three maids were all working for her. And they are her relatives. She spearheaded their recruitment when we dismissed the initial staff." He sighed. "She manipulated us all. All of them have been dismissed and will face justice," he assured her. "Mrs. Trowbridge played upon our fears and prejudices, making us believe Aunt Catherine and Maria were the villains. But the truth was far more insidious."

Letitia's voice broke. "I was so blind. I let Emily's words sow doubt between us. Can you ever forgive me?"

He cupped her cheek, his thumb brushing away a stray tear. "There is nothing to forgive. You were caught in her web, as were we all."

A small, tentative smile broke through her despair. "I love you, Philip," she whispered. "I could not bear the thought of never seeing you again. And if you will still have me, I should like to marry you."

Philip laughed. "Still have you? My dear, you do me a disservice. Of course, I will have you. It would be a terrible cruelty to leave you to fend for yourself, poor creature that you are."

She swatted his arm, a faint blush coloring her cheeks. "You are an arrogant swine!"

His grin widened. "And you, my love, are insufferably stubborn. A perfect match, do you not think?"

Before she could retort, he lowered his head, capturing her lips in a kiss that banished all doubt and fear. When they finally broke apart, he rested his forehead against hers. "You are mine, Letitia. And I am yours. Always."

Letitia's heart swelled as she concurred. "Always."

Chapter 30: Philip

The late morning sun poured through the tall windows of the Wynthorpe ducal estate's grand drawing room, painting the richly appointed space in warm, golden light. The room was a model of understated elegance. Silken drapes the color of cream framed the windows, and a pale green carpet stretched beneath chairs arranged for the intimate gathering. Philip adjusted the cuffs of his dove-grey morning coat, his blue eyes focused on the door as he waited. His hair, dark as the night sky, was neatly combed, and a faint smile played on his lips, betraying the anticipation he fought to contain.

Then he saw her.

Letitia entered, clasping the hand of the man she had called Father for twenty years. She was glowing like the stars as her white gown trailed softly behind her. The fabric glittered with every step she took, delicate needlework glinting faintly in the sunlight. Her hair was swept into an elegant chignon, with loose tendrils framing her beautiful face. Her green eyes found his, and her smile was a blend of nervousness and joy.

"My lady," he greeted as she reached him and Mr. Robinson moved away, "you look... utterly beautiful."

She smiled adoringly. "And you look... tolerable," she teased, though the sparkle in her eyes betrayed her jest. "No, truly, you cut quite a handsome figure today, Philip."

He chuckled, offering her his hand. "Coming from you, I shall take that as high praise indeed."

The vicar cleared his throat, drawing their attention. The small assembly quietened as Philip and Letitia turned to face one another. Around them, the gathered family offered warm smiles. Aunt Helen dabbed at her eyes with a lace handkerchief, her smiling husband standing by her side. Frances beamed at Letitia from across the room, her brothers looking suitably proud. James and Charles stood to his left with identical looks of satisfaction. Even Aunt Catherine and Maria, now allies rather than adversaries, wore expressions of genuine affection.

The ceremony was brief but no less meaningful for its simplicity. As Philip recited his vows, his gaze never left Letitia's. Her eyes shone, and he felt an unfamiliar tightness in his throat. This moment was not an obligation fulfilled, or a title secured—it was the beginning of a life he had never dared to dream he could have.

When the vicar pronounced them man and wife, Philip bent his head and kissed her. A soft murmur of approval rose from their small audience. The kiss was tender, yet filled with promise, and when he drew back, Letitia's rosy face made his chest tighten anew.

"I present the Duke and Duchess of Wynthorpe," the vicar said proudly, eliciting a round of applause from their families. They all surged forward to congratulate and hug the happy couple.

"I am so happy for you, Philip." Aunt Catherine embraced him with tears in her eyes before turning to Letitia with a broad smile. "You are the most beautiful bride ever, my dear niece."

"Thank you, Aunt Catherine." Letitia beamed as her aunt kissed her cheeks.

"Welcome to the family again, cousin," Maria inserted with a genuine smile, throwing her arms around Letitia.

Letitia giggled and hugged her tightly. "Thank you, cousin."

Philip looked on with warmth and gratitude that all the animosity between them was now a thing of the past. Aunt Catherine and Maria, having realized how they had been manipulated by Mrs. Trowbridge and how Letitia had almost died, had been filled with intense remorse. They had rushed to apologize to Letitia profusely and pledged their support and acceptance. Letitia, in her magnanimity, had readily forgiven them, joyous that they could now become a family. Although they were not close at the moment, they had become friends, and for that Philip was thankful. He had kept his word by providing them with one of his residences. Even though they acquired their share of the late duke's wealth, he provided them with an allowance. Maria had a large dowry that would definitely attract a suitor before the season was out.

"Congratulations, Your Grace," James teased as he clapped his brother on the back.

Charles drew abreast to hug him. "Thank goodness you listened to our counsel. I dare say your days of mooning in your study are over."

Philip chortled and shook his head, grateful for his brothers. James had gladly relinquished the title back to him, saying he had never wanted it because it was too much trouble. Charles had not wanted it either, not relishing the vast responsibilities that came with it.

As Philip looked at the smiling faces in the room, a sigh of contentment left his lips. Although they had had a turbulent beginning, it was all genuinely friendly now. Mrs. Trowbridge and all her cohorts were sent to prison, including Emily and Andrew for forgery and bearing false witness with lesser sentences. Letitia had been sorry that it came to that, as Andrew had apologized copiously to her. They had discovered the private investigator had refused to give up a name because Mrs. Trowbridge was his aunt.

As they did not know who could be trusted, they had let go all the servants in their London townhouse and replaced them with servants from Westridge and Brookstone. They had renovated the cottage in Westridge for Lucy and provided her with a monthly allowance.

Philip, in his quest to show Letitia that he was indeed not interested in her wealth even though she now believed and trusted him, had set up several businesses with half of the money. She had chosen to use the remaining half for various charitable ventures like building and renovating houses in Wynthorpe, Brookstone, and Westridge.

Philip came back to the present when Letitia slipped her hand into his. His eyes held her with immense love. They all moved to the ballroom for the wedding breakfast, and after the toasts and laughter subsided, Philip led Letitia onto the polished oak floor for the first dance. The string quartet began a lively tune, and he twirled her gracefully.

"You are quite the dancer, Your Grace," Letitia said, smiling. "I dare say your feet are grateful now that I have mastered the art of dancing without stepping on them."

He chuckled. "Ah, but you are the true talent here, my dear duchess. It seems being an heiress comes with an array of hidden skills."

She laughed softly. "And being a duke comes with a remarkable talent for flattery, I see."

He leaned in slightly, his voice low enough for her ears alone. "Not flattery, my love. Only truth."

She beamed from ear to ear. "I suppose I should thank you for allowing Aunt Helen and her family to stay here whenever they wish."

"They are my family now too," he said easily, spinning her in time with the music.

Letitia had given her family a sizeable part of her income. Her uncle was expanding his blacksmith shop and hiring workers, which allowed him more free time. His long hours had been affecting his health, and now he would not have to work so hard. Aunt Helen no longer worked as a housekeeper, and neither did her two sons work for Lord Bannerman anymore. Philip would see to their education. When they eventually returned to Brookstone—which he hoped would not be anytime soon—he would employ the entire family to supervise the charity work in the village. He did not wish for his wife to exert herself doing such.

"It is my pleasure. Besides," he added with a grin, "the estate needs a bit more lively company. Otherwise, it is just me, my beautiful wife, and a houseful of servants attempting to decipher my moods."

Letitia giggled helplessly. As they danced, Philip's eyes drifted to James and Frances, who had also taken to the floor. James held Frances's hand with uncharacteristic gentleness, and she smiled up at him with a warmth that suggested something more than polite affection.

"It seems my brother has found his match," he observed. "Wedding bells may soon ring for them as well."

"Frances deserves a kind man," his wife said with a smile. "And James appears to be a gentleman of rare merit."

He raised a brow. "Rare merit? You surprise me, wife. I thought you might wish for your cousin to marry someone a touch less... infuriating."

Her eyes gleamed with mischief. "Well, he is slightly infuriating, but in an endearing way. Much like you."

"Endearing?" He echoed the word with mock offence. "Is that the best compliment you can muster for me, my love?"

She tilted her head thoughtfully. "I could call you arrogant instead. Or obnoxious. Or perhaps a swine, as the situation demands."

Laughter shook his shoulders. "And yet you still chose to marry me. What does that say about your judgment, Duchess?"

"That it is impeccable," she re-joined with a cheeky grin. "I have managed to secure both a duke and a husband with a tolerable sense of humor. Few can claim such good fortune."

He laughed heartily. The music slowed, and the dancers stilled. Philip offered his arm, and they slipped away from their families, stepping onto the terrace that overlooked the sprawling estate grounds. They strolled along the gravel path, the soft crunch underfoot the only sound for a moment. Philip glanced at his wife with a fondness that belied words.

"You know," he said thoughtfully, "I used to curse my great-uncle for his meddling. The stipulation about the heiress seemed nothing more than a cruel jest at the time."

She looked at him with adulation. "I felt much the same about his will. It disrupted everything I thought I knew about my life."

He stopped, turning to face her fully. "And yet," he said, taking her hands in his, "I cannot be angry with him now. Without his interference, I would never have found you, Letitia."

Her gaze dropped to their joined hands, and then she looked back up at him, her eyes glistening. "Nor I you," she whispered. "I thought my inheritance would be the greatest treasure I would ever find. But I was wrong. *You* are my greatest treasure, Philip."

Her words struck him silent for a moment as he swallowed the thick bulge of emotion in his throat. Then, with a soft smile, he pulled her closer, his arms wrapping around her. "I have been called many things, but never a treasure," he murmured. "You are full of surprises, my love."

"And you are full of charm, Your Grace."

"Only for you," he breathed, lowering his head to capture her lips in a kiss. It was slow and unhurried, a seal upon the promises they had made that day. When they finally broke apart, Letitia sighed contentedly, resting her head against his chest.

"Do you think we shall ever find peace here after everything?" she asked softly.

Philip smiled and rested his chin lightly on her hair. "With you by my side, Letitia, I believe we can find anything."

Epilogue: Letitia

Three months later...

Letitia sat on a log on a grassy bank by the pond in the ducal estate. A soft breeze carried the scent of wildflowers, and the estate grounds spread endlessly in all directions, their manicured beauty blending seamlessly into the surroundings.

She adjusted the brim of her straw bonnet, the ribbons fluttering lightly against her cheek, and glanced at her husband, who was a picture of concentration beside her. He wore a simple white shirt with the sleeves rolled up, his dark hair slightly tousled from the breeze and his boots discarded near the bank. A fishing rod was firmly in his grasp, though the determined crease of his brow belied the leisure of their outing.

"Darling," she called tenderly, "you are gripping that rod as though it were a sword. Surely fishing is meant to be a relaxing pastime?"

He cast her a sidelong glance, his blue eyes glinting with amusement. "Relaxing? My dear duchess, this is a battle of wits and skill. I mean to catch the largest fish in this pond, and you shall witness my triumph."

She smothered a laugh, adjusting her own fishing line. Her gown was modestly pinned up to avoid any mishap, though she doubted its elegance would survive the outing unscathed. "A lofty ambition, darling. However, I fear you are destined for disappointment, for I intend to claim that honor."

He chuckled. "Then consider this a challenge, my love. Let us see who emerges victorious."

The hours passed in delightful camaraderie, their teasing and laughter ringing out over the still water. Letitia managed to snag a few small fish, her satisfaction evident as she placed them in the woven basket at her side. Philip, however, seemed to have a knack—or sheer luck—for catching larger ones.

"Another one!" he exclaimed triumphantly, hauling a rather impressive trout onto the bank. His grin was boyish as he held it up for her to see. "What do you say to this, my lady? Have you finally conceded defeat?"

She wrinkled her nose in mock indignation. "Hardly. I simply believe in leaving the larger fish to those who are in greater need of proving themselves."

"Ah, I see." He nodded solemnly, though his eyes twinkled. "You are sparing my fragile ego. How generous of you."

She burst into laughter, shaking her head. "Well, it is fortunate you have caught such a substantial specimen. It will serve nicely for dinner for three tonight."

He gazed at her thoughtfully. "Dinner for only the two of us, you mean. James and his betrothed cousin of yours, Frances, will not be joining us until the morrow, remember? And then two days later, Aunt Catherine, Maria, and her affianced will arrive."

Letitia's smile widened as she reached for the basket, placing her rod down beside her. "Two?" she mimicked innocently, brushing invisible specks of dust from her skirt. "No, darling. I believe three would be more accurate."

He frowned slightly. "Three? I must say, your mathematics eludes me. Who, pray, is this mysterious third guest?"

"My mathematics is flawless. When I say three, I mean three. In the Duke and Duchess of Wynthorpe's household. Philip Henshaw's family." She looked at him, her green eyes shimmering with amusement and something deeper, warmer. For a moment, she let the silence stretch, watching as the realization dawned upon him.

His eyes enlarged like saucers. "Letitia... Are you saying...?" His voice trailed off, replaced by an incredulous whisper. "You mean to say—?"

She smiled, her hands folding over her abdomen. "Yes, Philip. We are to have an addition to our small family."

For some seconds he was utterly still, as though the world had ceased to turn. Then his demeanor shifted to one of pure, unbridled joy. He surged to his feet, pulling her with him, and swept her into his arms.

"Letitia!" he exclaimed, his voice ringing with elation as he spun her in a jubilant circle. "You have made me the happiest and luckiest man alive. A child! Our child!"

She laughed, her hands clutching his shoulders as he twirled her. "Philip, put me down before you drop me into the pond!"

He obliged, though his grin remained irrepressible as he set her on her feet. His hands framed her face, his thumb brushing over her cheek. "You are truly remarkable," he crooned. "A duchess, a fisherwoman, and now... a mother. Is there anything you cannot do?"

"Win a fishing competition against you, apparently," she teased, though her voice softened as she added, "You will make a wonderful father, Philip. I can already see it."

He drew her closer, resting his forehead against hers. "And you will be the most splendid mother. Our child will be the envy of all, for they shall have you to guide them."

They stood like that for a moment, the world fading around them as they reveled in the joy of their news. Then, suddenly, Philip pulled back, his expression shifting to one of concern.

"Letitia," he began sternly, "what on earth are you doing fishing? Should you not be resting in your condition?"

Her laughter bubbled forth. "Oh, Philip. I am barely a few months along. I assure you, fishing poses no great peril."

"That is not the point," he insisted, though his stern demeanor was betrayed by the faint curve of his lips. "You ought to take better care of yourself. And I shall ensure it."

She raised an eyebrow. "You mean to watch over me like a hawk, do you? I pity the poor child already. They will not take a step without their father fretting."

"I call it vigilance," he replied loftily. "And you shall be grateful for it when I keep you both perfectly safe."

"Very well, Your Grace," she said with a dramatic sigh, though her smile remained. "I shall submit to your vigilance. But only if you agree to let me win our next fishing match."

"Let you win?" he repeated, feigning horror. "Never! I should be a terrible husband if I allowed such dishonesty. Our child must learn the value of merit, after all."

Their laughter rang out again, carrying across the pond as they gathered their belongings and began the leisurely walk back to the house. Letitia slipped her hand into Philip's, her heart brimming with contentment. As they walked, she glanced up at her husband, the man who had become her wealth, her inheritance... her everything. Yes, she thought, life was truly perfect.

"Thank you, Grandfather," she whispered.

The End.

Thank you for reading "Letitia, The Rightful Heir."

If you loved this book, you would love "Charlotte, The Case of Unspoken Love". Click link to start reading NOW! https://www.amazon.com/dp/B0F7Z1H4XT

If you enjoyed Letitia, The Rightful Heir, I'd be incredibly grateful if you left a review or rating. Even just a few words or a star raing can make a world of difference—it helps other readers discover the story and supports me more than you can imagine.

https://www.amazon.com/review/create-review?&asin=B0F2LCH7M3

Your thoughts truly matter, and I read every single written review with appreciation in my heart.

Thank you for being part of this journey with me!

https://www.amazon.com/review/create-review?&asin=B0F2LCH7M3

Printed in Dunstable, United Kingdom